Clear the road, here comes bandit!

You think the films were fun? Well put your ears on for Bandit's own version. It all begins when he's hauling an illegal rig full of 100% elephant. (Make that 200%—she's pregnant.) Sheriff Buford T. Justice wants that perpetrating pachyderm so bad he's going crazy, which Bandit helps him do across the South.

There's high-speed hijinks, fender-bendin' convoys, rip-roaring belly-laughs, and love. Bandit loves Frog, but she doesn't know it—neither does Bandit, until ham-handed Cletus fixes things up with a right cross.

And that's nothing compared to Bandit's crash-bang Coors caper—but why spoil the surprise?

THE ADVENTURES OF SMOKEY AND THE BANDIT

Delmar Hanks

Based on the Screenplays by
James Lee Barrett and Charles Shyer &
Alan Mandel, Jerry Belson and Brock Yates

Stories by Hal Needham & Robert L. Levy,
Michael Kane

BANTAM BOOKS
TORONTO · NEW YORK · LONDON · SYDNEY

THE ADVENTURES OF SMOKEY AND THE BANDIT

A Bantam Book / October 1981

Cover artwork and insert artwork courtesy of MCA Publishing, a Division of MCA Inc.

ISBN 0-553-20317-7

Published simultaneously in the United States and Canada

Bantam Books are published by Bantam Books, Inc. Its trademark, consisting of the words "Bantam Books" and the portrayal of a rooster, is Registered in U.S. Patent and Trademark Office and in other countries. Marca Registrada. Bantam Books, Inc., 666 Fifth Avenue, New York, New York 10103.

PRINTED IN THE UNITED STATES OF AMERICA

0 9 8 7 6 5 4 3 2 1

"Only boll weevils get blue slips . . . save the paperwork for the paperbag cases . . . then hang it in your ear."

BUFFER T. JIMSON (1929–1978)
(*Trucker and friend*)

To my mother.

Preface to Smokey and the Bandit

Certain adventure stories are closer to my heart than others. One such is *Smokey and the Bandit*, which some of you may have seen in the films. A man's story, but a woman's story, too. A story of high adventure on the road of life: human folly, love, and glory. The same old story, in short, a case of do or die.

In setting Bandit's record straight through a virtual stenographic transcription of his own words, I am aware that some may have some small difficulties with CB jargon. For that reason I have appended a brief glossary of all the most important terms.

Most Americans spend as many hours in their cars and trucks, buses, and vans as they do making love or exercising their bodies in other ways. In these days of soaring gasoline costs and vehicle prices, it's well to remember that saving lives is the business of all of us, Bandits as well as Smokies, and there are human beings everywhere. Love is never having to go to a drive-in movie in a Toyota.

My special thanks to Burl Milton Bandit for his advice and to R. Elman for his assistance in putting together these recollections.

DELMAR HANKS

El Dorado
Arkansas

THE ADVENTURES OF SMOKEY AND THE BANDIT

I

How It All Came About

When it came to filming my adventures, Hollywood, as usual, got it all ass backwards. What they said came first in my life came second, and vice versa. Leave it to those airheads to assume the pregnant elephant caper happened *after* we trucked all that Coors up to Texarkana in 24 hours on 18 singing wheels, when it was just the other way around, as you'll soon see, and that's so important that I think you should know. Who would go to all that trouble for a lot of chicken shit? There were human considerations involved, a lovely chick, a helpless female, and a 58-year-old extra-fat man name of Enos Burdette, and his son, the 12-year-old dwarf, Enos Junior.

What's more, there were certain other runs we made lickety-split, of a public service nature, that never even got told about. Like the time Snowman Cletus and me and his hound moved 20 tons of deadly poisonous radioactive waste up to Sandy Hook, New Jersey in a big lead thermos bottle for our local power company, and, of course, the only people who got exposed to all that Death right away was also just Cletus and me, which is why we could be so reckless later on, I suppose.

Then there was the time we moved all of some hotshot

politician's sectional couches from Austin, Texas up to D.C. in time for a big wingding. I was on cockleburrs all night long just to keep going. Shimmying and shaking—oooweee! Had the air blowers on full force to protect those plastic covers over the upholstery from a melt-down, and none of the taxpayers was ever the wiser for that. Lean on Bandit, and he's your man if you say just pretty please, and I'll also get you there on time, by bus, for sure, any day in the week.

Bandit, that's what they call me, and I look a lot like Mr. Burt Reynolds, in the pictures, only better, I think: a lot more spunk to my gunk, and I'm not just another pretty face. For a young spry guy I've been at it half my life. Little chicken-shit competitions here and there in the Southwest, and the big celebrity giggaroonios too, such as what I spoke of above. I am the man, especially when it comes to foxes, X-L females, I make their slappers go at high speed. But there are times when I lose all my mirth and turn melancholy, too, and whenever there is such a November in my soul I get behind the wheel of some big old rig and just floor it. Dig . . . ?

A lot of femmes don't understand this need to get away on my own, so I've become more or less of a free-lancer at such times, hiring out to Seven Brothers, the CIA, the Moral Majority, the High Y, the Amway, the Agway, and the Women's International Hadassah. Always for a price. Yup, I've seen it all, and eating peanuts off the bar, too.

Driving up through the South Bronx, once, late at night, with a load of Georgia fuzzballs for the Hunt's Point Terminal Produce Market, I've seen the Ladies of the Night in front of those big blazing bonfires flash open their satiny jackets to show they had nothing on but their belly buttons and hot pants, and would I like to help out a bit with the rent money?

Hell on earth never looked so good to me then, believe me, but I turned away. Never have cared much for the professionals. I'll show a lady a good time, but that's different. To show a lady a really good time you need lots of hay and lots of jack. Therefore I keep busy, moving Polish Hair Oil up from Tampico to Trash City, and once even a load of Crackerjacks in a big hurry to Miami. . . . But the two trips that really changed what's left of my life were the ones I mentioned above. Wouldn't you just know those typewriter jockeys out in sun-and-funland would get it all screwed up?

Putting shove before push, as they say, when in fact it was just the other way around: rights of the unborn before a mere trailer full of aluminum cans. Well, as we say down where I come from, when you got a bulldog sitting on your bonnet, you don't go nowhere for less than a dollar. So let me put the pedal to the metal and try and just motivate us.

How it all began: it was election time down in Texas. Mercy sakes. The mucky-muckies are always having us pick and choose some poor slob for public office somewhere in this blasted and doomed country of ours most days of the week, but the biggies usually take place sometime in early November, when it's still pretty much Indian summer in West Texas. That year in July the contest for governor was just getting underway between the two richest men in the whole darn state: Big Enos Burdette and Mr. John Conn: mortal enemies. Mr. Six-by-Six and the world's meanest hyena.

Mercy sakes alive.

When you've been chicken-fried in as much U-238 as Cletus and me was, you usually don't get it up anymore for politics or politicians. Fair's fair is all I really know. As old Lyndon Johnson said the day he died, the rest is silence.

So I was off by myself in my part of the state at my favorite pastime, of course, and Cletus was back home, too, also adding to his posterity. Sweet prince goodnight, but neither of us give a shit for either of those two vultures, Tweedledum and Tweedletwaddle, in duds by Sakowitz or Neiman-Marcus. But then that cunning little Charlotte entered into our lives, and plain went amuck with maternity, and it was just sort of difficult to be so laid back with all that happening. Eventually I'll explain. Just leave it to Bandit, 10-4.

So it was choose-your-rascal time in our part of the state and it was fair to heating up, like some old oil burner with a load of hanging beef. Out to the Panhandle near Big Enos' hometown of Burdette, the whale himself with his little pip-squeak, Junior, was standing up in the back porch of an observation car on a three car shortie on that railroad he'd run clear across the county from Cowtown, to address all his Mexican tenants.

Big signs everywhere, too: BIG ENOS BURDETTE—THE ANSWER TO YOUR PRAYERS ETC. BURDETTE'S SET. GET BURDETTE.

Everything but SCHOOL CROSSING and WILDLIFE PRESERVE.

It's one of those evil grim hot days when you can poach an egg in your own spit. Enos is really transmitting, a savage, big propane cooker: "BELIEVE ME WHEN I TELL YOU MY GOOD FRIENDS WITH ENOS BURDETTE IN THE CAPITOL IN, ER, AUSTIN THIS VALLEY, THIS VALLEY, WILL BE GREEN WITH THE FERTILITY AND FECUNDITY OF MOTHER NATURE'S BREAST . . . *I MEAN BEST* . . . AND OTHER MOST PROFITABLE CROPS. Blah blah blah . . . AND THIS RAILROAD I BUILT FOR YOU ALL WILL CARRY THE CROPS TO MARKET FROM YOUR LANDS."

"*Crap,*" cries a voice in the crowd. "CRAP PURE AND SIM—"

"WHAT'S THAT YOU SAY THERE, BOY?"

Big Enos is such a panty stretcher that when he bellows you can hear him from West Texas clear out to Sharktown, and not a word of truth to any of it. Best you can do is hang it on your door and pray for rain. So there was this one little cornshucker standing there at gunpoint with all his friends and he ups and tells Big Enos, "Señor, this isn't *our* land. You own everything from here to Locoweed Valley."

"So I do," Enos zaps him right back. "DETAILS, DETAILS . . . Put me in the governor's chair and we'll work that all out. Hell, I might even give you the land out of the goodness of my heart."

"Sure, when West Texas freezes over," says that brave Tex-Mex.

But Big Enos, he leans right over then, like he's got to spit, and whispers to Little Enos, "Then again I might not."

At that moment a faint drone was heard in the beautiful blue dusty skies of Texas.

Big and Little both glanced up, and over their own backyards and heading toward them, like they was Nagasaki, came these three great big World War II bombers. The big lone ones with high tails that look like big flying lizards, and electric shavers mounted on their wings. Real pieces of Americana . . .

Now for those of you who never set eyes on Big and Little, I ought to tell you those Burdettes were far from pretty to look at, even in the very best of times. The poppa bloats like the Goodyear Blimp, and the boy is just a chip off the old blimp, punky and blond. Not a pair of pretty faces for sure. Eyes the color of benny chasers, and a face on the old man like the front end of a Nazi go-cart.

Mean to look at, I'm telling you. Ugly as swinging pork, or their spit was the purest red eye; however, they can buy and sell just about everybody else in Texas between here and the dirty side; and what they can't afford, evil John Conn can.

And what do you know, as Little Enos presently observed, it was nobody else but that rich crazy son of a bitch John Conn up in the cockpit of the lead B-29, in a leather bomber jacket, crushed cap, earphones, like old Jimmy Stewart in *Thirty Seconds Over Tokyo*. On his face was the evilest grin you ever saw, as if he'd been keeping himself going strictly on grains for days.

So Conn, he spots the crowd down below, and he grabs the hand-mike and says, "Pilot to bombardier. Open up them there bomb bays. . . ."

"Bomb bays open," says the bombardier.

Down below Little Enos asks his daddy, "Are you thinking what I'm thinking?"

"Boy, it crossed my mind," says Big Enos. "But even a low down cur dog like John Conn wouldn't do such a thing. Hell, it'd be a violation of the articles of war. I'd report the sonbitch to the Confederate Air Force. . . ."

"Pilot to bombardier," says John Conn; then, high in the sky, "Bombs away!" he hollers.

And the doors open wide and out comes falling an enormous brown cloud of stinking cow shit.

Call it perfect saturation bombing: that stuff comes a-walloping and a-flummering and a-flopping down, all across that train and the entire neighborhood, dispersing the crowd but landing point blank on Big and Little Enos' ten gallon hats and ruffled shirt fronts. Just like they used to say about when it hit the fan. . . .

What a stink they made, I can tell you.

As he wiped a piece of dung off the tip of his nose with the end of his tie, Little Enos declared soggily, "Daddy, this bullshit has got to stop."

And going back home to base, John Conn is singing: "Make mine Country style."

Now John Conn was real fond of music. Aside from making money, it was his only pure unalloyed pleasure. He was pure Country. Texas crude. And he lived in a ranch house that made South Fork in Dallas look like a double-wide mobile home.

Oil was the secret; he had more wells than a dog has fleas. For mile after mile leading up to his front lawn it looked like a convention of praying mantises, with them big metal insects genuflecting like toadies up and down; and right in the middle of all that wealth a tall gold flagpole flew the Lone Star of Texas.

Conn could travel straight up to the moon on a stream of his own grease if he cared to, but he much preferred to go for more and more bricks. And in between he partied a lot to be governor and generally kept his own counsel.

The day after he had the sky lift its tail and drop those brown clouds all over Big and Little Enos Burdette, he was giving a barbecue at his spread for a few hundred folks, and the Rolls Royces were lined up for half a mile into the driveway, and the helicopter pad was almost as busy as the powder room with arriving guests. The Stadler Brothers band along with the Doobies were there to play "There Ain't Nothing This Side of Heaven" and some other hits; everybody was having a high old time; and John was stomping about on the patio buttonholing various of his guests. "I reckon if I toss in another hundred million or so," sez he, "I got this election campaign sewed up."

"Considering that you only raised $85 at your last fund-raiser, I'm afraid that's a matter of some dubiety, John," says one guest, who happened to be our present incumbent senator.

Just then a champagne cork popped, and down by the south 40 a gusher went shooting up skyward like a Titan missile with black gold galore.

John wasn't of a mind to pay any heed to business. He'd let the hired hands see to that; he was busy politicking. He says, "Down here we call that a Saudi soda. . . ."

"Plain wasteful," says the senator, "unless you got sponges."

"Not to worry," says John. "Heck, I'm no sponger," and he moves on to a pretty blonde who is doing the hustle with a visiting sheik from Abu Dhabi.

Says John, pouring himself a glass of champagne, "Here's mud in your eye . . . drilling mud, your majesty."

"Offendi," says the sheik.

"No offense," says John.

The band was playing "Abu Dhabu Honeymoon." Big chunks of beef were being skewered. "Abba Dabah Daba Daba Daba Daba, said the monkey to the sheik," sang the band, as if in total flattery.

Just then an ominous humming seems to make the whole sky vibrate and shimmy. The band falters. The sheik tugs at John's sleeve and points toward the heavens where these engine sounds are growing louder. "Allah be praised, you are expecting more guests, Sharif Conn?"

"Sheriff my ass," says Conn. "Not a damn chance. Those planes are just too small for my people. My people got things like DC-9s—decent size skeeters. But I tell you one thing, when I get to be governor there's gonna be some laws about damn fools like that flying low over other folks' properties. . . ."

"Inshallah."

Overhead a pair of powerful crop dusters broke through the overcast in tight formation. In the lead plane was, you guessed it, Big Enos, and he still had on that ten gallon shithat, and he looked real mean as he grabbed the mike and broadcast back to the second plane, in which sat Little Enos, similarly befouled: "You ready, son?"

"Nobody," says Little Enos, "shit-bombs a Burdette and lives to tell the tale. . . ."

"Let it fly, boy," says Big Enos. "LET IT FLY!"

They swooped so low over John Conn's ranch they blew the hats off some folk, and trailing after them was this really enormous spray of light orange Day-Glow paint.

Do you copy me? That stuff came down like falling rain and drenched the guests, the waiters, and about a million bucks worth of Rolls Royces. It spackled the entire band and turned Conn himself into Ronald MacDonald. In a rage he stomped about his slushy orange patio, and as the two dusters dipped their wings and sped away, Conn slipped in a pool of the stuff and fell to his knees.

"Inshallah, inshallah."

The sheik was also on his knees facing east and praying to Allah for deliverance from what the Heavens had splattered him with. But Conn was truly apoplectic. "Enos Burdette," he called out and wagged his orange fist at the sky, "your fat ass will never warm the governor's chair if I've got to spend every dime I've got. I'll get even with you, all of you, if I've gotta sell Kuwait."

"Abu Dhabi," went the sheik, correcting him.

"My ass," says John Conn.

A joke's a joke, but when the two richest men in the whole darn state of Texas start fussing and feuding and confusing shit for Shinola, that's the time for Government to exert its august authority, which is just what happened, of course: in July those two good old boys was called to Austin.

Governor Muff Deevers looked like a distinguished politician, excepting his wings of silvery hair had been dyed blond upon taking office, and he wore hand-tailored Sakowitz suits, string ties, and Paco Rabanne on both wrists, as well as on the bodice of his shirt.

An imposing figure as he paced back and forth in his office. When his secretary ushered in Big Enos and John Conn, she said, "Governor . . ."

"Call me Mark or Muffy," said the Governor.

Then he saw that pair of miscreants and changed his tune entirely: "You damn fools. Dragging our Grand Old Party through the mud—or should I say paint and cowshit—with your high school antics. Candidates for governor of Texas? Why don't you boys run for something a little more your size? How about Rhode Island? I understand Fargo, North Dakota, is looking for a mayor. . . ."

He sprayed the room with an atomizer of Paco Rabanne to rid himself of what must have seemed like their noxious odor.

"Have you ever thought about running a sanitation department in a nice small Montana town? I mean to tell you, you boys have made a terrible spectacle out of the honorable world of Texas politics. If I had my choice I'd endorse one of the Dallas cheerleaders before I backed either of you two turkeys. But you're the only two left. It's too late to choose anybody else. I'll tell you one thing, though. I am holding up my endorsement until one or the other of you can prove to me you've got enough sense to stop all those dirty tricks. Hell, you'd give the Watergate burglars a bad name."

Big Enos and John Conn were looking as contrite as Mormons about to go out missionizing, but Governor Deevers said, "Now get out of my sight!"

When they got out in the hall again, Conn went scurrying off to see his campaign manager, but Big Enos was so upset he just hung around, winded, leaning heavily against the heavy oak door.

Junior comes up to him then and he sees his poppa rolling his eyes like a gumball machine over the devastation that went on inside Deever's office.

Little Enos was about to say something consoling when they heard voices from the other side of the door. "Silsbey, I don't give a hoot about customs. I don't give a holler about quarantines. I don't give a goddamn about the Miami Port Authority. I have gone to considerable expense to obtain that gift for the Grand Old Party and I want it here for the convention. . . . It will be the symbol by which I, Samuel Houston "Muff" Deever will be immortalized as governor of this great state. I want *that* crate. That crate, Silsbey. Crate number 1444 that now lies smoldering in Miami, Florida because of your incompetence. Silsbey, get me that crate or I will make sure you get a job in the next administration which will doom you to public scorn, and probably a long jail term, regardless which of these fools replaces me. Now get me that crate. You've got nine days. Got it? Not get out . . ."

Talk like that is a commonplace among the types who rule us; those Watergate tapes were certainly no exception. They proved the rule, but Big Enos acted, as soon as he heard Silsbey ordered about and cussed out like that, as if it was all news to him and Spiro Agnew. He started down that hall like a lava flow off Mount St. Helens' volcano, and Junior was a rolling stone in hot pursuit. "Where we headed, Daddy?"

"To the governor's office, son. By way of Miami. We get us that crate 1444 and we've got the endorsement. That'll put that John Conn's ass in the tall grass for sure. You watch my dust."

Big Enos was beaming as if he'd been doused all over with fine champagne, not shit, and Little Enos was quick to seize his opportunity: "Daddy, you are going to make one fine governor. No telling where you'll stop. Chief executive, or who knows what . . . Always one step ahead of the opposition is what you are."

And then they skedaddled.

But they both didn't seem to be going in the same direction, because a few hours later Little Enos was shaking hands in the living room of John Conn's bright orange ranch house with his father's mortal enemy.

The only way anybody could describe that tremendous room is to say it was the epitome of tremendously bad taste. The walls were covered with stuffed animal heads, rifles, trophies, Texas and Confederate flags, and animal skins.

There were drilling cores fitted together beneath hand-hewn beams to make up the ceiling, and rugs of foot-thick synthetic bear skin, and on the wall above the fireplace, in which you could have roasted three large oxen, were three huge oil paintings: of General Douglas MacArthur; of Duke Wayne; and of John Conn himself wearing a pair of fleece chaps and two pearl-handled six-guns.

There were figures of Errol Flynn on a bucking elephant, with lariat and ten gallon hat; and standing busts of Rev. Jerry Falwell and Elizabeth Taylor. But, aside from the painting of Conn in chaps with his skin showing through, the most impressive work of art in the whole room was what I would call OLD GLORY MAY SHE WAVE FOREVER, which was a huge flag made of hundred dollar bills sewn together like a patchwork quilt, standing straight out from an M-16 rifle like a piece of wash in a very stiff breeze.

This was a singular example of the National Determination, I thought. Places like that should be photographed in color for *Barnyard Beautiful*, or *Better Homes and Pigsties*, if you copy my meaning.

Little Enos had come all the way here to double-cross his own pappy, and John Conn seemed to be extremely grateful for the visitation. He said, "Enos my boy, boy of mine Enos, I just can't tell you how much this little call of yours has meant to me."

And he kept shaking the pip-squeak by the hand like he was pumping oil.

"I sure do appreciate, for that matter, knowing about your daddy's trip to Miami. And I want to say this," he added, sounding very gubernatorial all of a sudden, as he patted the punk on his head, "you're gonna make this great and sovereign state one hell of a lieutenant governor. Now what was that sheriff's name again?"

"Sheriff Justice," Enos says. "Buford T.—as I recall . . ."

Conn let go of his hand and rifled through his notebook. "Funny, he's not on my payroll, but that's a minor detail. . . ."

He went over to the widescreen picture window and surveyed his domains. Fifty yards away a couple of ranch hands were sinking post holes. One of them put a post in place and, lo and behold, suddenly there was more oil. A gusher thundered up into the Texas sky.

Conn remained unperturbed. "Cap her off boys," he yelled out, "the storage tanks are full up. Besides, we got to hold on to it till we can make a fair profit on the stuff now that there's all that Mideast fussing and feuding. Hell, we ain't gonna give it away."

"Exactly my own sentiments," says Little Enos, but the next afternoon he was back with his daddy again in the family helicopter about to set down at the Atlanta Georgia International Raceway.

And that's how Bandit got into the story. Because it was

me they was looking for, even though I wasn't there, and all what came before this I later pieced together from the Snowman who was also on their minds. Old Cletus told me it was one busy day in Atlanta, or else he'd never even have talked to that pair at all after some of our dealings together; but the track that day looked like they were giving semis away for free at the main Peachtree Department Store.

Jam-packed with vehicles of every description it was, but the big semis predominated in the infield, and there was even a pack of diesel burners with bobtails racing around and around the speedway in one of the preliminary heats.

Big and Little headed straight for the garage area where all the semis were maintained. The noise was truly deafening, and they kept buttonholing strangers to ask directions but couldn't hear what was being shouted back at them.

Suddenly, Snowman's giant blue and silver GMC General rounded the corner of one building and rolled to a stop. Out of the tall cab stepped the Snowman himself. He greeted a few pals, and then he thought he heard his name being called, because he turned around and saw that gruesome twosome and started to turn away, but he reconsidered.

Snowman told me he greeted them, "Well, if it ain't Big Wart and Little Wart."

Huffy as always, Big Enos said, "Easy there, Avalanche. Us Burdettes don't take too kindly to slurs against the family name."

"Pardon me." Snowman grinned down from the heights. "Doggone if I didn't think you boys *was* a slur against your family name."

"Listen, Snowman," says Little Enos then, "we didn't come here to fight . . ."

"Boy you're smarter than you look."

Then it was getting down to business time.

For a leg up, Big Enos says they would ordinarily have stomped Snow right then, except they had a business proposition. "We need the Bandit," he says.

Snowman had figured that one already and said so.

Little Enos asked then if he knew where I was.

Snowman pointed out, "That would depend on how hard somebody was looking for him."

Big Enos wiped his brow of perspiration and said, "Mighty hard."

"As in *hard* cash?" Snowman asked.

"*Hard,*" Big Enos said, "as in 100,000 dollars, U.S."

Snowman *was* impressed. "You want his phone number, his Master Charge number, or the color of his jockey shorts?"

Just then the PA summoned all the trucks and drivers to the starting grid. Hearing his own name come out so loud over the pipeline, Snowman hopped aboard his own semi again and sat down. Sticking his head out the window, he told the Burdettes, "Better put those negotiations on hold. I got me a race to win. You boys just hang right there until we get back."

Then he put her in Mexican overdrive and really poured on the coal.

He had his dog Fred with him, of course, and when he came up to the green starter's flag he saw the competition: Big Red, Six Pack, Slow Poke, Hot Stuff, Small Wind, six other semis in all, with bobtails trailing in the wind; and Snowman, he took an early lead and never gave it up. Talking all the while to Fred about the high cost of racing etc., he went round and round that track, while the Burdettes watched, bug-eyed, as usual.

The prize was $20,000 after 200 miles at 118 miles an hour—not bad around the turns—and better yet, waiting for Cletus in Victory Lane was Miss Macon herself, Marlu Marmot. In her bikini and ermine cape, she was just about as pretty as any man could want to have when she leaned all the way over and accepted the biggest deepest soul kiss Cletus could ever give her. Then Fred, he wanted some, too, but Cletus grabbed him by the collar with one hand, and took his check from the judges with the other, and wobbled his way back to the running board of his semi where the Burdettes were paying court to him again.

Big Enos said then, "C'mon boy, time's a wastin'."

"Relax," the Snowman said, "as this is my moment of glory."

Then Little Enos asked, "Do you want the glory or the *beaucoup jack*?"

"That's easy," my friend said, "except for one thing."

Big Enos scratched his head with all five digits. "Let me guess. You forgot where the Bandit is."

"You got a winner," says the Snowman. "Damned if my mind ain't a complete blank."

"Well, let's see if we can jiggle your memory some," says Big Enos. "How's $200,000?"

"Those clouds are parting . . ."

"Two hundred thousand, take it or leave it," says Big Enos.

"Would you believe," he replies, "total recall?"

"Way to go, son. We'll have you counting on your fingers in a week." Big Enos scratched his nose with his ring finger. "Now here's the deal. You and Bandit have got to pick up a little package on the Miami docks and deliver it to the governor of Texas."

"Hey, that's heavy," says Snowman. "The governor, huh? I'd a thought he'd make himself enough sellin' judgeships and highway contracts so's he wouldn't have to be dealin' in that kind of *stuff*. What a shame."

"*No, not that*," the little shrimp points out. "This is strictly legal. . . ."

"Sure," says Snowman, "and you're Wilt Chamberlain."

"Ain't a damn thing illegal about this, I swear," Big Enos says. "I'll stake my reputation on it. His too . . ."

"Now that's what I call comforting."

Then Snowman, he tells them both the story of Simon Suggs. Seems Simon was somebody once lived down by Tallaposa Bend and he was fair to being quite a character; so one day his momma tells him the larder was getting pretty darn low, they was just about nigh out of sugar and coffee and not a dozen joints and middlings of beef or pork left, all put together, in the smoke house. So Simon he gets on his old green army blanket overcoat and orders up his horse and within five minutes he was off to a camp meeting.

Well, he found this hollow square of people in a grove near a swamp fair to filled with rattlers and shakers and others making great evangelical and pentecostal exhortations, and he got right in the line of sight of the preacher who, when he saw him like that, asked Simon if he had also been redeemed.

"Redeemed? Whoever said I was a Green Stamp?" he snapped back.

"Brother, don't mock me. . . . Do you wish to be born again?"

"I mock you not," said Simon, "if the Lord be not with me I'll . . ."

He stopped himself short with a glimmer of the eye, and then he let the fit take him mighty powerful, worse than most, and he startled just about everybody by rolling about and thrashing around. "O LORD LORD LORD AM I A SINNER AM I EVER . . ." And so on and so forth. "Free at last free at last," he writhed and writhed. "Born free and so on and so forth."

Well, he went at it for more than a few hours until sunset and all the people was standing about mightily impressed. They held Simon close and fed him soup and bathed his sweaty brow and made him rest from his exertions; and then he was calmed again and rested and allowed himself to be baptized right off; and afterwards the preacher and Simon agreed it would be best if he went back to his creek in the piney woods and built a church of his own for his mother and their friends, and to that purpose they took up a collection and pretty near to $200 was raised in ones and twos.

The preacher then said, "Now hand that over here Simon and when you need it I will come and bring it to you for your church."

"I think it best," Simon said, thinking fast, "if I go right now with that into the swamp right down there below and bless this holy collection as the Lord above has commanded me in my heart just now to do . . . for he said, 'Take it to a swamp where it is damp.' "

"Hear, hear," cried the onlooking congregation.

And so they gave Simon the money and he turned and ran into that swamp and never come back out again until he was home with his ma down in Tallaposa Bend.

"Now what do you think of that?" Snowman grinned when he was finished with his story.

"What be the meaning of that piece of folklore?" asked Big Enos.

"Well," says Snowman, "just like Simon, it sure as hell makes me feel a whole lot better, believe me, knowing who I'm dealing with. Do you copy me?"

"Takes a thief to know one, poppa, is what he means," says Little Enos.

"More like don't hustle a hustler," says Snowman. "Don't kid a . . ."

"Either way," says the little punk. "Any day . . . One more thing though—we heard some stories about the Bandit slipping . . ."

"I believe the exact phrase," said Big Enos, "was down the tubes."

So then Snowman didn't take his own advice because he told them both, "That man's in better shape than the day he was born. Cross my heart and hope to die if he ain't."

Read on, dear reader, and maybe you'll be able to make your own decision as to whether that was true or false.

As my own mother used to say, "When the wind is north-northeast, I can tell a hawk from a handsaw."

II

What I Was Like in Those Days

One of my favorite songs of all times is "Ozark Fraulein" the way Eddie Arnold used to sing it. You remember, don't you? This soldier was in Germany and he met a pretty fraulein there and when he left she stayed behind and he missed her something awful because she'd become his Ozark Fraulein.

What a sad song that was.

Fraulein, Fraulein . . .

Golly. I'll tell you one thing I know, for sure: it's much better to sing sad songs, or hear sad songs, then to be in one yourself. And that's just the way I was feeling myself: sad and lonely. Love sick.

> "*Dear Bandit,*" an Ashville, North Carolina woman named Flo once wrote to me in care of the Alabama State Highway Patrol in Montgomery, "*if you will endeavor to send me the measurements of either your foot or your hand or both, I will attempt to knit you socks or a pair of driving gloves.*
>
> "*Only the foot or hand sizes are necessary and desirable, thank you. No other details.*

"A fine man like you must keep his extremities warm and cozy. Take good care of yourself, Bandit."
Flo Onslager

Such letters from solicitous, lonely females are sometimes even now a commonplace in my life.

Plenty of women I could have had but what I wanted I couldn't get. You know who I mean, the Frog. She'd done gone and left me. I had it bad and that wasn't good. . . .

Here's the way it all happened.

That girl passed me in life just once on a run out of Swabby Town but she damn near blew my doors off. You see, she was *the* woman of my dreams, and yet I picked her up, as I recall, just outside Bogaloosa, Louisiana running from her own wedding in a white gown and veil. Bodacious . . .

She rode with me, wherever, I can't recall, and by the time it was over she went back home to her momma, but I was so mad in love I couldn't believe the thump-thumping of my own valves. Try as I might to distract myself from thoughts of my little Frog, she was always in my mind and heart, even when—for example—Snowman finally found me competing in the Celebrity Olympics in Palm Springs, California.

What a scene that was.

Lots of big names were on hand: Nick the Greek, and Howard Cosell, Cheryl Ladd, Norman Fell, Jerry Lee Lewis, Donny Osmond, Diana Ross, and yours truly, Bandit.

As master of ceremonies, that eminent sportscaster and humanitarian Cosell did all the interviewing. I'd been drowning my sorrows in barley pop for three days straight and after the potato-sack race, while Cosell was putting it to Cheryl Ladd about why they lost and how, I got my legs tangled under me right on camera before 50 million Americans.

Cosell was saying, "Cheryl, can you in any way attribute your sickening defeat in this key event in the competition to the aromatic aromas of 'fix' that has pervaded the arena since these games began?"

Well the only aromatic aromas I could detect were me, myself, and I when I came out from my dressing room to get made up, but Cheryl took the hype from Howard and stuck it right back in his nose: "Are you suggesting these things are rigged?"

"I am only telling it like it is," says Cosell, as my feet just then got caught in a coil of coaxial cable and I tripped and fell and collapsed in a heap right behind Mr. Cosell's right shoe. Luckily, there were two network clones who saw my pratfall, and, as the camera panned the playing fields, they picked me up and dragged me back into my trailer.

It was there that the so-called wonderful transformations of stardom began for me, all over again. They made me suck in my gut and fastened me inside a corset such as my Aunt Selma used to wear for Sunday going to meetings only. Then they applied so much mantan and pancake makeup to my poor hungover face I felt like the mocha divinity cake Aunt Selma used to bake for after services on the verandah.

Then they had to pry me inside this flashy skintight set of duds, with two shoehorns just to fit my ass inside those pants, and I was draped all around with so many gold and turquoise and silver chains my head was pulled down into my chest and drooped slightly more than it should have. The boots were from San Antonio, a $300 pair, made out of elephant hide, would you believe, and it took three of them to push each one across my ankle. When I was all dressed, and pomaded, and ready to go live again across the good old U.S. of A. into millions of folks' homes, I missed my cue and burst out of that trailer and onto the scene while Cosell was still interviewing Ms. Margaux Hemingway about her granddaddy who was some kind of big-game hunter.

Ever unflappable, Cosell said, "Well, well, Bandit. You look like Steubenville, Ohio after they closed the steel mill. The field was rife with rumors that you wouldn't even be able to make today's competition."

I belched up some sour beer and swallowed hard and mumbled, "In the pink, Howard."

"And every other color of the rainbow, too, I see," says he, as I staggered and almost fell again. "But," he adds, "we really haven't seen too much of you on the celebrity circuit this year, Mr. B."

I mumbled something about wanting to dust his breeches with the front end of my Trans-Am, but I doubt if any of that was carried coast-to-coast, and Howard actually seemed to keep the upper hand. He was actually giving me the brush-off.

With elaborate breezy cool, Cosell pointed out, "Would you say your brief fling as a celebrity was based on the shattering of a multitude of sacred laws of our land? That you are a speed-crazed, thrill-hungry hoodlum with a reputation for public inebriation who deserves his status as an unknown anonymous nonentity?"

All I could get out was, "Oh . . . sheeit," though I was thinking to myself: nice way, buddy, to talk to a brother with radiation sickness.

I mean, I carried that waste to the Sandy Hook for all of America, not just me, and now America was treating me like plain common trash, and I was acting that way, too.

Cosell turned to the camera then, as if I wasn't even so important. "And now, ladies and gentlemen, we pivot our attention to a pivotal moment in this epic competition . . ."

"*Eppes a* competition?" he added, then, as an afterthought.

I hope somebody laughed at him because he was plain trashing me. The camera zoomed in on the starting gates, and I was propped there like a big sunflower, waving my cowboy hat at the crowd. But nobody waved back.

I got up on the top rail and disappeared into the box, my legs straddling right on top of this big bristly sow.

Stank too, real hard, so I asked the starter, when I was ready in place, if he had anything to drink. Such as some red eye.

Cosell's voice came over the PA: "This contest will be decided by the first contestant to traverse the 50 yards and cross the finish line aboard his mount."

The starting bell rang, those gates snapped open, and ten of us good old boys thundered toward the cameras towed by our pigs.

You see they was mounted with harnesses like Seeing Eye dogs, and we were harnessed to each pig and wearing roller skates. As soon as the first gate opened they started dragging us so that chaos commenced, and some were dragged, run over, stepped on, but not me. Not Bandit. *Nosiree* bub. I had prepared me a long stick with an ear of corn dangling from the end of it, and with that corn hanging just a few inches beyond the porker's nose at all times, I was trundled straight and true to the finish line, winning easily, whereupon she got the ear of corn and I, among other things, got a spattering of pig pie all over my new elephant skin boots.

Needless to say, even Cosell was impressed with that performance. You couldn't hear yourself think for the applause and all his adjectives: "Amazing . . . an amazing exhibition of pigmanship by the Bandit. Here is a man of humble beginnings, a virtual unknown, martyred to the worst sort of radiation sickness, a mere trucker triumphing against some of the immortal superstars of the country-and-western world, and of TV.

"A startling development," he went on, "and now the world is asking, has the Bandit seen the light? Is he ready to enter the world of responsible citizenry? Only time will tell."

Well, after all that praise and all that exertion, I patted my pig and went over to get my prize and fainted dead away in the mud.

They put me up in the Gator Motel. Seems a doctor had examined me and he said radiation sickness hell, boy, all you got is a bad case of piles from driving that truck, and he prescribed a lot of Preparation H and bedrest in the motel. Well I was feel pretty relieved, of course, but I wasn't feeling too good otherwise because it was so goddamn lonely for me still, and I started in to drinking again, and had pretty near finished off one whole bottle when Snowman showed up with Big and Little Enos.

(Getting over all the fear and all of a whole year believing I was gonna die was certainly some of it, but there were also other things, too. Like Frog. I still missed her powerful. And no amount of substitute chicks seemed to help out.)

When Snowman came by I was sitting up drunk with my scrapbook meandering down Memory Lane. I could hear their voices outside my window before I even saw either of them. Little Enos spoke first, "You call this dump a motel?"

"Seclusion," my friend Cletus explained, "so's he can get away from the mobs. . . ."

Truth was I'd had so much red eye by then I could have

grown corn in my stomach, and I was just about half-hearing and seeing things, too

Big Enos says, "Let us talk to him."

"No, no," Cletus says, real slow and persuasive, as he ladles out his words at random, like a calf kicking at yellowjacks. "You two wait right here. I ain't even sure Bandit will want to see you. . . ." Like a man laying bricks so that every one fits. "I got to clear it with him first."

"Why is that?" asks Big Enos.

"Man, we ain't talking about Enos Salts, or just anybody," the Snowman explains. "I'm talking about the Bandit, half-man, half-horse, half-alligator, and all heart. He's got a lot of action, like a dog has blood-sucking ticks, and he's probably busy sifting all the offers right now. . . ."

Truth is I was just about to splash my way into darkness one final time until morning. The tears were rolling down from my eyes like acorns from a blind hog, and when I heard that knock on the door all I could say was, "It ain't locked. Ain't even closed . . ."

Then I saw Snowman and his brother. At least I think I saw two of them, but only one came over to shake my hand and hold me steady when I got up out of the chair to greet them.

Snowman says, "It's only me from across the sea, Bandit. How's it hanging?"

"Great. Like a tick under a cow's belly. Just great. Couldn't be better. Fabulous."

But it was too much for me. I collapsed against that table and started pounding that scrapbook with my fists. "Snowman, how could Frog leave me? When I loved her so?"

"So what?" My old friend turned sarcastic like he was soaking old socks in lye. "Probably didn't have anything to do with those three weeks you spent at the Mustang Ranch chasing strange fillies as if it was the last roundup. Or the time," he went on, "you pinched the senator's wife at that White House reception, or the way you was blowin' in the ear of the Orange Bowl Queen on national TV. Nuthin' like that, I reckon."

Teach me to open my big self-pitying mouth in front of

Snowman who really knew better. I picked up that scrapbook and turned to a photo of the Frog and me alone on a beach, waving. God, she was pretty. She looked just like Sally Field. Mopsy and cute.

"We had such good times," I told him.

"A young woman like that never needed all your trouble, Bandit," Snowman told me. "She can get all the troubles she wants free-lance. . . . Anyway, what you need, good buddy," he added then, "is a nice friendly widowed woman. One that is real sensible, steady-going, never-skearing, never-kicking, willing, spirited, a smooth pacer."

I couldn't follow a word he was saying, and I told him so, and then he says, "You just leave it to my old woman and me. We know some nice widow girls you would really enjoy getting to know . . . not to mention a divorcee or two. . . ."

But I was all eyes for those pictures of me and Frog, and when I looked again it was a picture of that time in Astro City I won a trophy and I had one arm around Frog and my other arm around the judge. "I took her everywhere Cletus," I opined. Then I turned to another picture of me winning another trophy and this girl in a bathing suit was leaning over to give me a big kiss mouth while I still had my arm around Frog. "We were so inseparable."

"Maybe so," says Snowman, "but three's company . . ."

Another picture and this one shows me surrounded by The Stadler Brothers with Frog off to one side.

Still another shows me with a bunch of Vegas cuties, and they're well sort of semi-nude, in bikinis. Poor Frog's head is just barely in the photo, as she just barely manages to peer out from behind the tallest showgirl.

I showed that one to Snowman and said, "Doesn't she look cute here?"

"Where?" was all he said.

So then I pointed her out to him. "Right here. Damn, we had a good time in Vegas."

"Bandit," he says, "I can see you're still torching for her because you're singeing my dog Fred's ears out in the truck, but if you think that sweet little girl was having fun watching you make an ass of yourself . . . you're . . ."

Then he stopped himself short as he is like to do and snapped his fingers together. "Now wait a minute," he says. "I ain't got time for this now, and neither do you. Sober up Bandit or I'll drop you into a vat of tomato juice. We got two prime suckers out there willing to pay us a ton of money for a little driving job that's really next to nothing. . . ."

"Driving?" I said like he was speaking another language to me. "Where?" I grabbed old I.W. Harper and took another belt. "I don't drive any more. . . . No more . . ."

"Shhhh. Don't say that," the Snowman said. "Big and Little Enos are standing out there in the cold ready to give us $200,000. Now suppose you just sit there and help me take it from them," he finished.

I was slurring pretty badly. "What do you want me to say?" And I slipped down off my chair.

Snowman propped me back up again and said, "Just you sit still, Bandit, and don't play with yourself, or nothing . . ."

"*Play with myself?*"

"What do you call it?" Snowman said as he went to the door, and with a flourish of his hand swung it open and let in Big and Little.

He put a finger up to his lips. "Come on in gentlemen, but don't talk too loud. He's meditating . . ."

"*Om*," I went. "*OM*," trying to make it sound like my mantis as I had learned with Frog that day she took me to her TM class. OMMM.

No help there. My brain was fogging up. Better to sit still and try to concentrate on what Cletus was pitching at me. "Bandit, you remember Tweedle Dumb and Tweedle Dumber. Well, they now have an offer for us that you will probably want to consider refusing. . . ."

I nodded, but just that sudden motion tilted the chair so I slipped out sideways from it against the floor. Then Snowman hurried over and propped me back up again.

"OMMM," went I. "OMMMMMMMMM."

"Don't give me that, Bandit," Big Enos said. "It be a real sweetheart of a deal. Two hundred thousand skins just to take a certain package from Florida up to Dallas."

"Hmmmmmm," I said. "OMMMMM."

Big Enos added, quickly, "Not good enough, huh? All right, $300,000."

I couldn't focus, not even on that scrapbook. Like my eyes were BBs. All I could think was, all I could say was, "Ffrrogh . . ." like I was gargling on my own garble.

Big Enos must have thought I was being stand-offish, too, because he immediately raised the price another hundred thousand. "You got it," says he. "Four hundred thousand dollars, a deal . . ."

He took me by the hand and gave it a big shake. The big hello and good-bye too. "Got to be off now. I'll be seeing you boys in Texas. Here's the number of the crate."

"Number 1444, Miami," my friend the Snowman recited aloud. They started to exit, those two, but Snowman was good with the footwork. He said, "Ain't you two forgetting something? Wait a sec."

"What would that be?" Big Slobbo asked. "What now, boy?"

"M . . . O . . . NEY," sings Snowman.

"Boy," says daddy to his little squirt of a son. "Boy . . ."

"Yes, daddy?"

"Give 'em some traveling money."

"Righto," says Little Enos, and he reaches into his pocket for a wad the size of a good size plug of red man burleigh and forks it over to the Snowman. "We'll give you half now and half when you deliver. . . ."

"Half my ass is what you mean," says Snowman. "Whatsa matter? Don't you trust us?"

"Righto," says the pip-squeak, "so we'll give you half now anyway." And then they left us, like a one-night stand on a country road.

I mean, they disappeared right out of the front door of that motel, except, I later learned, that when they got outside, Big told Little he was a real yoghurt brain if he thought his daddy was taking him back to Dallas right away because he was to stay around and keep an eye on us two and all that money.

Little Enos was one mean-spirited little punk, and he said, "Daddy, snitching on other people is kinda out of my line of work, but I'll try. . . ."

"Thanks sonny boy," says the old man. Then, "You may be stupid but you're also loyal."

Then Big Enos drove off in his limo and Snowman and me we just sat around trying to get our heads together. He was shaking me so hard by the shoulders seemed like I was having a fit. Little did I know until much later that as soon as Big Enos drove off the boy got on the phone to John Conn at the ranch, person to person, and you can just imagine what they had to say to each other.

Meantime, Snowman's shaking me down like a thermometer and waving big wads of greenbacks in front of my eyes. "Great job old Bandit, old Bandit . . . Come on now Bandit, us good buddies just got to hit the road."

"No way," I'm telling him. "I can't do it."

"Sure you can. This money is the one thing that might truly save your ass and somebody's got to drive lookout for Smokey."

"But I . . ."

"Ten-four, good buddy," says the Snowman. "We can do it. Easy as three-five. One mo' time, you and me against the world . . ."

"World without *amen*," I said then, and passed right out in that chair, while Snowman was saying, "Help, somebody help. I'm gonna get help."

Pretty soon I was seeing lots of sugar plum smokies along that long long trail a-winding to the girl of my dreams. Then I started to dead-head and went out completely, a total blank.

III

Sugar Britches I'm Calling You

In a quaint little white-washed church on a tree-lined street in Texarkana, squeezed in somehow between a 7-11 store and the parking lot of a Rickel's Home Outlet, wedding preparations were, meanwhile, taking place.

The church was called "United Evangelical Fundamental Church of God, The Twelve Apostles, and Assorted Saints," but a piece of the last part of the sign was so weather-beaten it read ". . . sorted Saints."

Well, anyway, on that joyous day in that toodling town the Man himself, Sheriff Buford T. Justice, pulled up behind the wheel of a shiny brown police vehicle with more lights than a Christmas tree, and sirens and static sticks galore, and from the passenger side out jumped a fresh-faced eager young airhead in a tuxedo and boutonniere—Buford's son, Junior.

The boy ascended the steps to his own funeral, as we say. Then out steps Buford Senior in the sorry flesh, wearing his dress uniform, complete with medals, a cap with a scrambled egg visor, rope piping on the tunic, epaulets, a brace of pearl-handled pistols, and a big chili stain on the meat of his left jodhpur. If you didn't see the stain, you'd probably have thought he'd been outfitted by none other than the late General Douglas MacArthur himself. He's so flaky looking, carrying his dark-braided leatherettc swagger stick, and he is in an unusually happy mood for a Smokey to boot.

"*Smile awhile and kiss me satadoo,*" sings the Sheriff, in his wheezy tenor. As he steps outside that car he is greeted by a smiling blank-faced couple on their way to his boy's wedding.

"What a fine day for a wedding like this, Sheriff," said the female of the pair, who happened to be called Ida May. "You must be mighty proud, sir—having such a wonderful boy like you got and all. . . ."

Being complimented on his boy, rather than for his own splendor, made old Buford instantly grumpy. "The hell you say. Boy's got his daddy's good looks but his mamma's brains," adds he, "which ain't none at all. Trying to marry the same floozie twice!" (Cause, as you recall, she'd run away from Junior that first time when I'd picked her up and fell head over heels.) "Ida May," says Buford then, "if we wasn't standing here on sacred soil I'd boot his scrawny ass all the way to Wichita Falls. . . ."

"That's a lot closer than Snyder or Rosenberg, or one of those cowtowns," she says, "but I understand, Sheriff Buford. I remember. There was that trouble time number one. All that business with that poor child bride being abducted by that . . ."

"*Abductor,*" says her boyfriend.

"Lothario," adds Buford, as the beeper inside his jacket begins to sound off like he's swallowed some tiny little Sputnik or something. "Errol Flynn. Ravager and rapist," Buford adds, winding himself up tight like a fist, "in the most innocent sense of the word, of course . . ."

"O yes indeed, that awful man," says Ida May, as the Sheriff's beeping increased in volume. "What *was* his name?"

Sounded like the Sheriff was about to explode from his own inner time bomb. All he could say was, "Bas . . ."

"O yes, the Bandit, of course," goes Ida May.

Sheriff Buford T. Justice looked so pale he could have been his own bedsheet. Lips quivering with rage, he slapped at his beeper as if it were a fly in his belly button and flinched at the pain he'd just caused himself, and yet the beeping sounds grew even louder, coming then in clusters, more like hornets than mere flies.

Ida May said, "Excuse me, Sheriff. That noise . . . You got some kind of stomach complaint, or is your radio acting up?"

"My new radio *is* a stomach complaint," says Buford, as he squatted on the sidewalk with his two hands over his head, mumbling sounds like "OOOM, OOHOOOM," as if he was trying to transmit something, too, on that tiny waistband receiver.

Presently all the beeping quieted down, as if they'd given up on old Buford for today, and he got up from his knees again, looking weary but flustered, not quite so splendid as before.

Buford says, "Speaking of the wonders of science and so on and so forth, that beeper's my new hemogauge. It tells me when the old ticker's getting upset. Feller from down in Florida perfected it to measure occupational stress in the workplace and so on and so forth.

"Well, so then," Buford T. Justice went on without any letup, "I have to relieve the stress with this special exercise developed in a monastery high up in the Hindu Kush. I bought my hemogauge from a very reliable old firm of Hindus in Oklahoma City, Oklahoma. Thirty-eight hundred dollars, tax included, and they give you an instruction book, too. I guarantee it's worth every penny. . . ."

"Just so long as *they* guarantee," says Ida May, "it seems pretty wonderful. Must make it so much easier for you to deal with that awful business about your new intended daughter-in-law running off with that awful handsome Bandit."

Soon as my name was uttered aloud one more time, Buford's beeper went real crazy, and the Sheriff had to crouch down and begin all his weird Hindu Kush noises again. Meantime, inside the church, the pipe organ commenced to play the wedding march from Lowenbrau Junior Buford stood at the altar. And then my own, my Frog, started down the aisle. She was wearing white, for respectability's sake, and she looked so pretty in her full-length gown like a bunch of walking apple blossoms, with only two children, a ring bearer and a flower girl, to accompany her.

I wished I could have been the bearer of something else up to that altar.

Standing in her pew in the midst of that crowded congregation, Ida May made a stage whisper to the fellow next to her, "Ain't it a shame she's wearing white and don't she have anyone to give her away."

Frog reached the altar and knelt a moment before rising again as the organ stopped. The crowd was all oohs and aahs. She started for Junior, a look of certain distaste hidden by her white veil, and then people in the church heard the phone ringing off in the vestry room. Wouldn't you just know it was Junior who went off to answer it, polite as a never-you-mind to old Cletus himself, my good buddy, who was on the other end. . . .

You see, as soon as Cletus had gotten me at all sobered up, I started begging him to get in touch with Frog right away before it was too late, because I wouldn't take on this gig no way without her.

Snowman pointed out, as he had before, she might not be too anxious to see me, but I said tell her anything: I'm dying, beg her if you have to, or you can just go without me.

So Cletus got on the tube after a while and tracked her down to the church. We're standing in this motel room waiting for Frog to come to the phone and Cletus can hear her telling Junior, "I don't think I should take it."

So I say to Cletus, "The only condition I want is her to come along on the job."

"What's that I hear?" asked Junior.

Falsetto, Cletus hollers into the phone, "This is a first priority call from the First Lady herself . . . in the White House . . ."

"Honey," says Junior, "you better come and take this . . . it's the White House. Long distance . . ."

"For me?" She's mighty impressed. So she goes to the vestry room and picks up the phone as Junior goes outside and tells the minister and all the witnesses and the congregation, "Just a minute folks. This is important."

Now you could have heard a bomb drop it was so quiet, and seems like everybody in that church can hear Frog speaking into that phone: "Yes, I am. O . . . hi. Cletus? Kind of busy right now. Whatsa big idea? *Who's in trouble?* O yes . . . I remember *him* . . . my help? Why should I help him? Radiation sickness? Don't give me that one, Cletus. What's that you say? . . . Fifty thousand dollars, Cletus? Yes . . . that is a good reason . . . I'll be right there. . . ."

She hung up and rushed right over to Junior whose carnation was beginning to shrivel and wilt on his lapel. "Darling," she asks, "do you love me truly?"

"Golly, sure I do, Carrie," says he.

"Then you'll understand," she says, "because I'll be back . . . and when I come back I'll have the money for that quadraphonic milking machine you said you wanted. . . ."

He's so dumb he's even gullible. Says, "Righteroo, Carrie, if you say so, and someday we'll even get us a cow. . . ."

"Maybe a whole damn bull," she says, as she kisses him and starts to run down the aisle.

But there was the Sheriff blocking her. "Where do you think you're going?"

"The ladies' room," says Carrie.

"Don't feed me that one girl . . ."

"Alright, Sheriff, the truth is," she says, "Bandit needs me. . . ."

Buford was like to have a coronary thrombosis. Tilt went his eyeballs and then they started twirling in opposite directions. He grabbed for his chest so his decorations started popping off.

"Ban . . . Ban . . . Ban," says he, as his beeper begins to whinny like a nag, and he can't even stop it with more "oohhmm oohhmmms."

Frog is just about to sidle around him, but she had owed him one for a long time. "Sheriff, I'm real sorry about this," she said. "I mean, *real*, but we'll just have to hold things up a little while longer. Nothing to do with Junior. He's really a wonderful boy. . . ."

She picked up her skirts and started as if to make her move. "And," she added, "sir, I've got a feeling you'll want to get some fresh batteries for your beeper."

Jeepers creepers. Frog went right out of that church in a big hurry, and jumped inside that waiting car with the "Just

Married'' signs, tin cans, and garlands. She revved up those engines and just fired away, leaving a trail of black rubber smoke. Before you could say Pine Bluffs, Arkansas she was jamming down on the bootrest and hammering her way down through Texas.

And when she was out of sight, that little wimp Junior emerged on the curb in a cloud of his very own postponed bride's dust. Some folks was throwing clouds of rice at him, so it shouldn't go to waste, and it flaked the shoulders of his tux like heavy dandruff. Coming toward him he heard the beep-bee-BEEP-BEEP of his dad, Sheriff Buford.

The boy says, ''Damned if I didn't think I was going along with her daddy.''

''Damn your hide boy,'' says Buford, only you can't hardly even hear him for his beeping and those ''ooohms'' he was articulating to keep his blood pressure in check.

IV

Throwing a Shoe

A few years back, they had a show on the TV with chimps playing real people. They did everything like people except talk. Their lips were synced up through animation. There was an M.C. who interviewed chimps from every walk of life: a doctor, a chimp on the street, an undertaker, a mechanical chimp, and they all answered his questions. What do you think of Nixon? Reagan? The new Polish Pope? *War and Peace*? The bomb? The ERA? It was very popular for a while. I think they called it "Planet Of The Apes."

I felt a lot like one of those chimps waking up the next morning in our motel room with such a dry mouth someone would have had to draw it in just to get my lips moving again.

Right away I reached beneath the motel bed for my can of Bud, but Snowman, still working on keeping me sober, had emptied out the suds in the can and replaced them with dark sweet java.

"Don't you know caffeine is bad for my health?" I told him and found a can he hadn't tampered with.

"Bandit," he said, "the shape you're in, you ain't got no health."

He started pacing the floor.

"This training program I set up for you is a big bust. At the rate we're going, Big Enos could ship his package to Texas by third-class oxcart before you'll be ready to run."

"What about Frog?"

"She's coming," Cletus said. "It takes time."

I thought of Frog again and something went all soggy inside of me. The woman had sentiment. I was sure of that. It wasn't only the money she was coming for. Still, I couldn't be positive.

"I still don't understand why you asked her to come," I told Cletus. "I don't need her. Don't need anybody."

"You sure seem to need that beer pretty bad," he said, as he came across the room and pulled the can from my hand.

He was in an evil and cantankerous mood, as if he'd had enough of my temperament to suit him for a long long while.

Sitting on the edge of his bed, he peeled an orange in one long swirl and offered me a segment.

I refused, of course.

"C'mon Bandit," he said, "why don't you just admit you're glad the Frog is joining us here? Hell, you're gonna need all the help you can get to be in shape for this joy-ride."

"I throwed a shoe Cletus," I said. "My life has sprung a flat. How's she gonna be of help? She's never been much of a help to me before this."

"Cause you never let her be."

"I loved her."

"Yeah, and you pushed her right out of your life." He picked up my scrapbooks again. "You think that poor girl was having fun? Look at these photos. She had to get in line just to see you."

"She ran off when the going got tough," I pointed out.

"No," Cletus said. "You pushed her away when the going got good. And remember what I told you. I told you if she ever left you'd go right in the toilet and become a boozy ex-superstar."

Bandit downed his beer, and belched, and grinned. That's me, of course, but it seemed I was so drunk I could even watch myself doing it. "See how wrong you were?" I asked. "I told her of the battles I had fought, and of the men who wore their heads beneath their arms . . ."

"Aw cut it out, Bandit," Cletus said. "You ain't nobody's hero now."

I belched again, and like I had just flicked on a switch somewhere, a light crossed the motel window, catching Snowman's attention. He went over to it and looked outside.

"She's here at last," he said. "Good God almighty."

I rushed for the door.

Outside the night was thickening. It was full of mosquitos and crickets, flies, chiggers. Balmy, you know, with vapors from the nearby petroleum cracker. The motel sign winked VACANCY, and the lights of Carrie's car dimmed and went out.

I kept my distance as she stepped into the darkness.

"Hi," I said.

"Hi."

She stood in the dark, a shimmering ghost of beauty. Her white gown glistened. She had removed the veil so that her face was flushed in the light a single overhead bulb glinted down on her from the motel roof.

Surveying her outfit, I said, "You're looking . . . good."

"So are you," she told me, with her eyes on my paunch.

"Boy, sure been a long time since we seen each other," I said. "Six or seven months maybe . . ."

"I think it was more like 8 months and 4 days," she said.

"Well," said I, staggering, "missed you, I did, but otherwise I been doing just great."

Carrie couldn't hide her smirk, part compassion, part scorn. "Been following your life in the *National Enquirer*, Bandit."

I was angry. The libels a man has to live with once he gets a certain reputation are enough to turn the soul sour. "Don't believe all the stuff about me selling my blood to buy booze," I pointed out, "and as for Lillian Gish, I never dated her either. . . ."

"I'm sure you didn't," Carrie said. "That great actress has better taste."

"Taste?" She had me there. I wanted to change the

subject. I was curious about her. "Where did you go after we, you know, split up?"

"After we split up," she told me, "I went strictly to pieces, one piece at a time, and it took a while I might add. So then I went up to New York, New York, and I started dancing again. I even got a good job. I was in the chorus line of *Annie* until I got fired."

I asked what happened.

"I couldn't get along with the brat," she explained.

"So then?"

"I went to work in a rock musical: SOCK IT TO ME BACKWARDS."

"Sounds great," I said. "Is that where you got that dress?"

"What's wrong with my dress?" she asked.

"Nothing," I told her. "For a musical . . ."

"Just because you dress like Hopalong Cassidy," Frog said, "doesn't mean you're still pride of the ranch. . . ."

I didn't want any trouble. I was just so glad to see her I had to admit I was. "No more fights," I told her. "I'm sorry, baby. What'd you want to tell me?"

"I didn't want to tell you anything, you big bum." Her face was flushed. She was peeved with me again. So beautiful the way she looked when she got angry. Just the way Momma used to look when I was a boy.

"So," I asked her, "in the musical what did you end up doing?"

"I played a razor blade," Carrie said.

"A what?"

She explained there was a nightmare sequence where she danced out dressed like a straight razor. "My dancing stunk," Carrie said, "but the music was great, super. I fell in love with the composer. He was *the* finest, bravest, most positive man I ever knew."

"Oh great," I said. "What happened then?"

"He killed himself."

She was sobbing and trying to keep herself from showing. I couldn't help myself. She moved me deeply, more than any woman I'd ever known, and I had to show her that.

I came up close to her and hugged her gingerly, patted

her back. But she pulled away and ran to Snowman who was standing nearby, threw her arms about him, and gave him a big warm sisterly hug and a greeting. "Cletus, I'm so glad you're here. . . ."

Then I saw a corner of her veil poking out of the crack in her suitcase. "What's all this?" I asked, abandoned, holding up a swatch of that gauzy stuff to the light.

Carrie said, "Didn't you tell him, Snowman?"

"Just slipped my mind I guess," Cletus said.

Carrie said, "If it's any business of yours, Bandit, I was all set to marry Junior when you called and got through to me."

The only word for what I felt was pure unadulterated outrage. Junior? That was like marrying a clothing-store dummy. Maybe something in the undertaker's window?

"How," I asked, "did you wind up with that turkey again?"

"Loneliness," Carrie explained. "A woman needs tenderness. He came to New York for a lawmen's convention. I was having my hair done in the lobby of the hotel and he saw me there, under the drier, and he came running up to me and gave me a big hug, curlers and all. Well you know it just felt safe," she went on. "Maybe because we were surrounded by all those badges."

I said, "You sure found a whole lot of fellas to cuddle up with once we was splintered."

"You were finding gals," Carrie pointed out, "while we were still together."

It hurt to have her speak so sort of truthful. I said, "Carrie, let's not waste time finding fault. A watched pot never boils, and a fool and his honey are soon parted. The important thing is we're back together, just like you always wanted."

I leaned over again and gave her a big kiss, which she seemed to enjoy at first, but then she backed away again, saying, "Lookit here Bandit, my bucko, let me make myself clear as the driven snow. I ain't your honey anymore, and I'm certainly nobody's pot. I am a free and liberated woman, a supporter of the ERA, and opposed to all male chauvinistic swine such as you whenever I happen to make their acquaintanceship. Now whereas I admit," she went on, "there was a certain modicum of physical attraction between us and even some residual affection primarily due to nostalgia, my main reason for being here is financial. M-O-N-E-Y, like Jello, so now let's get started putting your ass back into shape. . . ."

A flower from the big chestnut tree overhead was dropping scented petals onto what was left of the night, and when some fell lightly across Carrie's shoulders, she looked more beautiful than ever before, more or less like a great big beautiful blossom herself. I knew she still loved me. I just knew. Don't ask me why . . .

But you couldn't tell a thing from the way she and Snowman treated me over the next couple of days.

They could have made me eat toads and it would have been no worse. Up at six, milk, juice, more milk, and chickory coffee. Then walking and jogging ten miles every single day while Carrie toodled along beside me in a golf cart.

Every time I tried to sneak a can of beer I got caught red-handed. The penalty was ten push-ups. I was made to lift weights, and do sit-ups with Carrie's foot resting on my stomach. Pumping iron one day I felt this tear all down along my back. There wasn't any pain, and Carrie said it was "all the beer suet getting ripped away."

They made me practice my driving in a penny arcade bump-car arena, and when my reflexes improved a little they switched me over to a fork-lift truck down at the airport which Snowman rented from some Mexican contractor. I'd drive smack into a pile of sandbags, lift and carry backwards full speed in reverse, then turn around and start all over again.

Boring, but sort of sexy, what with Frog as my taskmaster. Most evenings, I was strictly up for Zs-ville, so there was very little chance to try and fool around. Once, coming back to our motel after another hard day of training, I felt older than Muhammad Ali after he fought Holmes, and yet Frog and Snowman seemed very happy with my progress. She said, "Bandit, you're getting to be your old self again."

"Old is the word for it," I said, patting her in the caboose. "Ain't it just so."

"Well, I have to figure out if that's good or bad," she said, her voice raised an octave suddenly.

"It's good," I said, exhausted.

"Good for you maybe," she said, "but a girl like me has got to watch herself."

"So watch." I patted her again.

"Cut that out," she said fiercely.

And Cletus said, "Bandit I think you should leave for Miami in the morning. Your driving is as good as ever."

"What am I gonna leave in?" I asked. "Sure wish I hadn't sold old Trigger. Shit, I need a drink . . ."

"Guess we'll have to show him," Frog said then.

"Looks like it," added Cletus with a shrug.

He smiled at me just like Santa Claus. "We've got a little surprise for you, good buddy. Step outside."

Parked between the Coke machine and automatic ice maker was a beautiful brand-new shiny black Trans-Am with white walls and wire wheels, twin pots, and leather seats.

I couldn't begin to control the evil smile that crossed my face.

"Where was that we're going?" I asked.

"Miami," says the Snowman.

I walked all about my new machine and caressed its flanks and fenders and long sinewy lines and tail fins: a woman is one thing but a good car is all that it's cracked up to be, and more.

Going back inside our motel room afterwards, I was all smiles. Little did I know that Little Enos himself had been hiding behind the mechanical ice maker, and when I went inside he ran to the nearest pay phone and called Mr. John Conn and left a message on his service: "Bandit's rolling."

V

The Double Nickel Near Dead End

We cruised on down through Florida at 55 mph, with me in the Trans-Am, and Snowman and Frog in the semi. Going at the double nickel through those little towns and hamlets of the Florida Panhandle we must have been a truly incredible sight to those state highway patrolmen. I guess they expected us to be streaking, but we didn't want to step on the bear's toes until we had to. So they'd aim their radar guns at our convoy and get a digital readout of 55. The speed limit. You could say we were just loafing along until we had our cargo. Then we'd hit the pedals and scram back up the state again. 4-10.

In Miami it was drizzling on the day we arrived: big patches of cloud in a blue sky, and the wind brisk, too, like rattling ice cubes. As we wound our way through Cocoanut Grove toward the dock area of Miami, with Key Biscayne stretching out like a big green finger into the Caribbean sea, Frog (who was sitting with me now) said, "You're doing well old pal," and she wound her arm around my shoulder so I was like to get the shivers.

We pulled up by a guard shack at the edge of a giant warehouse complex. In the background I could see tiny white-caps on the water, though the rain had stopped. There was a huge ramp used for loading cargo. A chunky guard with one of those fake replica magnum brand pistols, and a thick cigar between his lips, came out slowly from his shack to greet all of us, "What you boys need?"

Then he saw Frog and doffed his cap and added, " 'Scuse me ma'am."

Carrie giggled playfully. "Just think of me as one of the gang, officer."

"Yes ma'am." He doffed his cap again and turned to Snowman in the cab of the semi. "What's up big fella?"

Cletus said, "Got us a pick-up to make for a Mr. Enos Burdette of Burdette, and Austin, Texas. Crate number is 1444."

The guard nodded and waddled back to his shack to check his clipboard. "He looks to me like that mechanical bull they got at Gilly's in Dallas," says Carrie to me then.

I shushed her right and proper.

The guard was still within spitting distance. He held up a clipboard full of swindle sheets and rifled through the various invoices and bills of lading. But he didn't seem able to find #1444.

Then he took one of the drawers in his desk and dumped it all out and, as the papers started flying about, he grabbed off each one and read and rejected them, too.

Pretty wild way to do business, I'll tell you. Like when the shit hits the fan he's got to be in the middle to know it's even happening. Our little trio looked on in amazement. But he finally found the paper he wanted.

"Here it was all along," says he. "Got it right here. It was right in between crate number 1443 and crate number 1445. You want to go down to the first building on the right, and then hook a left. First dock on the left."

"Right," I said.

"No, left," he said. "You want to go down here to the first building . . ."

Snowman gunned his engine. "Don't worry, we'll find it," he said and off we both went.

But, suddenly that guard leaped out of his paper storm of a hut and started chasing us down where we were parked, right alongside this steamer from El Salvador, sort of a banana boat, I gather, because it was loaded with peelback crates of U.S. tanks and artillery.

As we stepped out of our vehicles to perform a little first echelon maintenance preparatory to taking on cargo, this warehouse bear is shouting at us, "Hold it boys. I can't let you take that crate. No way . . ."

He's waving that fake gun in our faces.

"What daya mean?" asks Snowman.

"I just checked my records another time," says the guard, "and that crate's in quarantine for another three weeks."

"*Quarantined?*" Snowman was pretty dubious. "You mean our crate's got measles? You must be joshing."

"Ain't no place in the security business for joshing," says the guard. Some papers had been blown out of his shack and were floating around by his cuffs. He picked one up and rejected it, and then picked up another and another. "I got it right here somewhere. Just you hang on. It's probably still stuck on my spindle inside. . . ."

Another paper floated across his face and he grabbed for it. "Now there it is in black and white: 'Hold for quarantine by U.S. Customs.' It's a custom, boys. . . ."

He laughed at his own stupid joke.

I said, "Listen mister, we got to have that crate in Texas inside three days . . ."

"Well," he laughed, "no harm in taking the crate, I suppose. It's just that you'll have to leave what's in it here for another three weeks. Bye now," he added and went back inside his shack to put all his papers in order again.

Walking back to our vehicles, Frog asked, "Is that what y'all call freight yard humor?"

I shrugged. It was all news to me. I turned to Cletus. "Old Bean, is there something about this deal that you're not telling us?"

"Bandit, I swear on my mother's innocent son's blood, Big Enos said it would be there waiting for us and would fit right in the truck, no problems."

"No problems?" I repeated, because it was certainly weird, and I'd known all along there was something weird about all this.

We were standing by the cab of the semi with Frog

seated in between us on the running board. "What do they quarantine anyway?" I asked. "Horses?"

"Cows?" asked Frog.

"Rabid parakeets maybe," scoffed Snowman.

"Jumping beans," I put in.

And Frog volunteered, "A flea circus?"

"This doesn't make any sense," I said, finally. I was slightly peeved at the Snowman, as you can imagine. "I only know one thing," I went on, "it's going to take more than the U.S. Government to keep us from getting that crate to Texas."

"Terrific." Frog with her damn scruples again. "I hear they've just remodeled Leavenworth. Boy, you get healthy one day and then you're racking your brain to figure out how we can spend three concurrent life sentences together."

I needed a drink quick, and I said so. But Frog said it would have to be coffee. "That's what I meant to say, coffee," I told her.

We went and had some, and a little mouth-to-mouth resuscitation, too. Later that evening in the dark we came back with a big flashlight and I scaled the fence and opened the gates so we could sneak our way back to the warehouse.

Afterwards, Snowman held the flash and he was very sparing about using it, just poking it here and there, with a blast of light, and then off again. We probed among the crates and cartons and located crate number 1443. So we were getting close.

But number 1443 was only the size of a liquor crate. Next to it was a monster box which towered almost to the roof.

I thought it must be the wall and said, "There isn't anything next to 1443."

"Nope," said Snowman, panning his light along that monster crate, "nothin' but this damn wall."

"Wait a minute," Frog pointed out. "Cletus, shine that light way up there again."

Cletus scanned the light beam upward and numbers and strange lettering appeared. Immense painted numbers which the beam of the flash picked up one at a time: 1 . . . 4 . . . 4 . . . 4.

And the lettering was all squiggly and wiggly, like maybe Indian or Arab.

Cletus asked, "Why would they paint the numbers of our crate on the side of a building?"

"That's no building," I said, in the middle of a brand-new brainstorm. "It's just a crate that's acting like it was a building."

"I was afraid you'd say that," Frog said.

"Well," I said, "here's where we start to earn our money."

Whatever there was inside that crate might have been half horse and half alligator, with maybe just a little touch of the snapping turtle.

As Snowman and I started to hammer off the fastenings over the latch, I remembered a drunken dream I'd had only a few weeks back in which I was wrastling with a critter such as that, big as Lookout Mountain, and covered with grease. A bear of sorts, without a squad car, and just as I had pinned the damn thing down, one of its greasy paws struck out and took my face away and I woke up.

Just thinking about that critter of my dreams again, so vast and evil-smelling, made me crave strong drink, a slug of the Lightning or Jeremiah Weed. But Frog would never hear of that, I knew, so I decided to badger my friend Cletus just a little again. "Suppose you tell me that part again," I said, "about how easy this will be to load onto the truck."

He took it all in his stride, with a shrug. "I'm only telling you what Big Enos told me, Milton," which was the first time anybody had ever called me by my first name. "Can I help it if the man is a habitual liar?"

Frog was all wisecracks, too. "No wonder he's running for governor . . ." Then she glanced over at me: *"Milton?"*

"It's Milt to you," I said, "or Bandit. Either one. Guess which I prefer?"

The lock snapped and the three of us inched open those giant doors onto a pitch darkness which even the flashlight could hardly penetrate when I got up close to it. "Cletus," I called out, "bring that damn light even closer."

"Hurry up," Frog said. "It will be daylight soon."

Just as Snowman and Frog came up close with me to

peer inside, the air was filled with an earth-shattering inhuman roar.

I grabbed Frog and pulled her to one side.

"Good creeping craphoppers," shouted Snowman.

The doors burst open. There was a clatter of large clodhopper feet and a shunting of powerful weights against the sides of the crate.

"Lord love a duck," said Frog. But it was certainly no duck she was talking about.

This ten-foot-high elephant came charging out, trumpeting and waving its trunk about wildly.

It looked at first like the world's largest vacuum cleaner, but it kept advancing on me with a considerable menace, I thought, until it caught me with its trunk and flipped me high in the air in a double somersault so that I landed in a crouch on its back. Then it started to run amuck through the warehouse, smashing crates and equipment as if they were so many matchsticks.

Well heidy ho, I thought, as I just hung on. That elephant was making debris everywhere and then charging about in it. I felt terrified, but I wouldn't let on I did.

The great beast seemed like it wanted to shake me off its back right onto the waiting prongs of a John Deere fork-lift, and I screamed, "NOOOOOOOOOOOOOOOOOOOOOOOOOOOOOOOO . . ." Frog and Snowman, who had been chasing after us, stopped dead in their tracks when they heard my scream and charged toward the other end of the warehouse, as far away as they possibly could.

I felt a lifting of the whole back end and then air beneath me, and I fell what seemed like a hundred feet or more against the floor, with a thud.

The animal, meanwhile, was standing perfectly still, with one of its big feet raised in the air, as if on show.

I got up and brushed myself down for broken bones and bruises just as I heard Snowman and Frog searching for me. "Bandit, where are you, boy? You okay?"

The beam of their flash made bright spots in the dusty atmosphere.

Coming up wide behind the elephant, I said, "Sure I am. Still in one piece anyway."

I was tucking in my shirt and straightening my hat. "Caught me a little off guard," I told them, "otherwise I would have rode the critter the full ten seconds."

"Just before you disappeared," said Snowman, "I thought you had him rode."

"Will you two get serious?" It was Frog again, standing next to Cletus in a swatch of bright dust motes. She pointed to the beast. "I think Jumbo over there has a sore foot."

She came closer to examine the foot.

I grabbed for her. "You crazy or something? That's a wild beast. A jungle predator . . . born killer. Better let me handle this."

She backed away, impressed, and I moved forward cautiously. A slash of direct sunlight fell across the warehouse floor as I peered at that enormous round circular foot.

It was morning.

We'd have to get a move on pretty fast.

What I saw was a nail the size of a Lucky Strike sticking out of the callused underpart of the foot. The beast must have speared itself in that wild stampede out of the crate.

I held the foot with two hands steady as you go, and then took my good right hand and gave a sudden yank. The nail came easily free, and the elephant trumpeted with relief and pleasure.

That wasn't all. It wrapped its trunk around me and lifted me off the ground and swayed from side to side, like a gigantic pile of chocolate pudding.

Frog said, "That's a love dance, if ever I saw one."

"That thing's just 'bout the size of my Aunt Charlotte," Snowman added with amusement, "and she even boogies like her, too."

Frog said, "Charlotte would be a good name for her, Cletus, as she's obviously one of my sisters, if you know what I mean. A female." Then she turned to me. "While you're dancing, why don't you waltz her into our van and we'll get this show on the road before we're caught."

Atop the elephant's back, I felt smaller and punier than I'd ever felt, even though I was no longer scared of her. "Be a good girl," I urged Charlotte, "and put me down . . ." But she kept on dancing. It was the story of my life all over again. I can turn 'em on, but I can't hardly turn 'em off afterwards.

Then Frog came up close and said, "Back off Charlotte. I got first pick on Bandit. He's mine."

And what do you know: she stopped her clumsy two-step and sat me gently down with her on the ground.

She let me lead her by the ear to the truck and deep inside. Snowman was worried about all the noise we'd made, but I pointed out not to worry. The sailors from the ship were all on shore leave. That guard was a drunk. "And they'd probably think it was something minor anyway, like an earthquake or a refinery explosion."

As we closed the doors on our pachyderm guest of honor, I told Charlotte, "If you need anything sweetheart, just whistle."

VI

Stepped On

I guess I never figured Charlotte would tap right back at me, almost bursting open those doors.

Then, again, I never figured on a lot of things that bright sunny morning in Miami.

As we headed out of the shipyard toward the gate and the exit, I told myself, "Healthy little devil, ain't she?"

Then I came to an immediate screeching halt.

Blocking the exit was this police car from Texarkana with Junior Justice at the wheel and Sheriff Buford T. standing beside it, mike in hand, ready to make us welcome. I suddenly had the feeling this was going to be a very long exhausting trip.

Justice seemed to have just about the biggest grin on his face I ever saw when he spoke into the mike: "Mr. Bandit, as you can plainly see, there is no escape. I intend to see that the law gets its sweet revenge. I figure 20 years will be about right for a son-bitch such as you."

Frog—I could see from my rear view mirror—was in shock in the truck. Wasn't there anybody anywhere she could rely on? But I kept fairly cool all the while, like a cockroach munching a crumb.

I had my own mike inside the Trans-Am and I told

Buford, "You make me such a tempting offer, Sheriff, I think I'll jump at it."

Then I hit the pedal medium hard and started out. There was a ramp for unloading cargo standing next to the gate and, when I got within ten yards, I touched the floor and that Trans-Am took off in high and jiggled and golliwogged a second before sailing right up through the air, like a fish taking bait, and over Sheriff Buford's sedan.

I touched ground again rear wheels first and over my intercom I could hear the pulse of a beeper, and then Snowman said, "Hang on Fred, Froggy. Here we go."

Looking back I saw Justice sitting with his hands over his head, expecting to get blitzed. Looked like he was praying, too, as Snowman's semi approached the front end of that bear sedan and slammed right into it, spinning and sliding it like a hockey puck on ice some 30 feet or more, before heading out through that exit door.

Maybe it was a good thing we'd practiced in that penny arcade after all, because we were on the lam again. Out through Miami Harbor and along the coast road and down toward town, with Justice trailing us a limping quarter mile behind. We kept spinning around corners and going up alleyways, blind corridors, and boulevards of bare brilliant sunlight. Pretty soon we were in a part of town where the only building looming on the horizon was the Orange Bowl stadium and all roads seemed to lead right into it.

It was a Sunday afternoon and the parking lot was jammed with cars. There was a constant noise of cheering rising up from its innards, as if the place was some kind of holy sanctuary which I, indeed, now took it to be.

I went right in through the main gate at 40 mph just at the moment of half-time between the Miami Dolphins and the Pittsburgh Steelers. Thank the Lord most of the players were already off the field, and the band and the cheerleaders were just about coming on to do their thing. As I skidded along the perimeter on two wheels, I glanced up and there was my old buddy, Mr. Terry Bradshaw, looking astonished, as if he's been tackled by a steer.

The Sheriff's car with its battered front end was just barely peeking inside the stadium, and Snowman and Frog had pulled up in their semi right along beside. That crowd was going crazy. A big cheer followed by a "locomotive steamroller Bandit" shook the stands and the scoreboard began to light up with wild, milti-colored signals:

GO BANDIT!
STAND ON THE GAS!

I called out to Snowman and Frog, "Hold on folks, I got to say hi to a friend."

"A cheerleader friend, no doubt," said Frog.

"If this guy's a cheerleader," I told her, "women's lib has gone too far."

Rolling to a stop alongside Bradshaw, I added, "Terry my man, what's shaking?"

"Footballs, baby," he says. "Bandit, what have you been doing? I haven't seen you since the year . . ."

"Don't talk Hollywood," I told my old pal. "Fact is," I added, with a certain charming false modesty, "I've spent most of my own time of late becoming an international celebrity, making movies and stuff."

"O yeah?" Bradshaw seemed unimpressed. He picked up a football and tossed it clear down the field about 80 yards. "Sorry I missed them," he told me then. "I ain't into stag movies, old buddy."

"Not to worry," I said glibly. "Listen, don't think a thing about it. But you can do me a favor."

"Name it," he said.

I pointed at the smashed front end of Sheriff Buford T. Justice's sedan. "That pair of crazies," I said, "pretending to be police officers in that wreck over there, have been hassling me something wicked. I'd really appreciate it if you'd have one of your boys delay them for a while so me and my child bride here," I pointed right at Frog, who was frowning back, "can get some peace and quiet."

"For you, Bandit, easy as creaming succotash," says Bradshaw. "Anything . . ."

"You're a prince, Terry," I said. "See you in the Superbowl."

"Park your car if you're coming," said he, and he

beckoned immediately, as I drove off, to Mean Joe Green from his own line and said, "Joe . . . those guys in that junker are giving the Bandit bad breath. You want to lay a little muscle on them?"

"You want them membered or dismembered?" asked the mountain of muscle and bone.

"Nothin' radical," says Bradshaw. "Make 'em think of God a little . . ."

Well, by then, I had my foot poking through the floorboards on the tarmac again and we were blowing out a lot of wind, but they told me Joe just stood right in the path of the Sheriff's car like a traffic cop, and when the Sheriff came to a stop right by his feet, threatening to make him into an Astroturf sandwich, Joe stood glaring at him.

"Hey meatloaf," says the Sheriff, "out of my way."

"Daddy, that's Joe G . . ." says Junior.

But he don't pay him a no-never-you-mind. "Clam up. I can handle this turkey." He tells Joe, "Move it, bubble gut, or get ready to get run over."

"That's been tried before," says Mean Joe Green. "Believe me, present statistical data gives you a very low probability for success."

The Sheriff allowed as how all these dumb jocks were big, but dumb as a stump.

"Be your stump daddy, and mine," says Junior.

Then, or so they told me later, in one swift graceful move, Mean Joe Green bent all the way over, grabbed one corner of Buford's junker, and flipped it over onto its roof.

Junior and his dad were hanging limply from their seat belts, like big sides of pastrami.

"I was trying to tell you, Daddy," goes the boy, my rival, "that's Mean Joe Green."

"Now you tell me," Buford says. "I thought he was one of the cheerleaders."

Then Bradshaw gave the high sign and Joe just flipped them both back over again. As soon as he was upright, Justice leaned out of his front window and said, "Thanks, Mr. Green, a very neat little trick. Real fun. We'd like you to do it again sometime. Maybe you could visit us sometime in Texarkana and try that on the mayor's car."

He drove off to applause from the crowd—for Joe, not him.

But as he was leaving, I picked him up on my CB as he was telling Junior, "If I get him inside the Texarkana limits he'll be in the slammer until hell freezes over."

Then he noticed his press-to-talk was on, I guess, and he spoke into the phone directly: "This is Sheriff Buford T. Justice. I'd like to call Canada . . . person to person, Mr. Belvedere . . ."

"Daddy," asked Junior, "who be that?"

"Be your kinfolk boy," says Buford. "Our kin. Not that I need the help. It's more a family reunion than anything. But I sure hope Belvedere puts his shoulder to the wheel and gets here pronto."

"You said it, Daddy."

"Quiet Junior."

I had a good ten mile jump on them and I was pulling away fast.

VII

Pedal to the Medal

Alligator Alley in the Glades was my destination and I got there so quick I did slow time for a while with the Snowman dragging on behind me in the rig.

Beautiful country, full of pelicans and white egrets standing on magnolia boughs, and all the while I drove I thought about that time in Memphis with beautiful Sissy Pomoff at the Peabody Hotel Lounge when we two-stepped to old Willie Nelson. That was in the good old days before Frog ever came on the scene. Sissy drank sloe gin fizzes and she liked to rub up against me hard when everybody else was still at arm's length. Called me Pandit Bandit, and she was real pretty, too. Then, after Frog, I was in soil bank a long while and couldn't even look at another woman. Wished she was with me now, but she was all the way back there with Snowman and Charlotte, not taking any chances on my charm.

So, because I had nothing else to do, I started to sing to myself, a song my momma taught me when I was a little kid to put me to sleep:

Mister Froggy wenta courting and he did well
O ho O ho

* * *

"Ain't no Mister Froggy in my life," said Carrie then into the CB burner. "None at all. Now you stick to business."

"Righto," I said. "How 'bout that, Snowman? You got a copy?"

Old Cletus' voice came back so filtered it was like he was talking outta some other orifice aside from his mouth. "Bandit, you just caught the Snowman flooring. Just jumping down that Alligator Alley, don't ya know, until you passed me by like rolling thunder."

"Eyeball your mirrors," I told him then, "and tell me what you see."

"Clean and green," says the Snowman. "But I also foresee a lot of trouble if I don't find me a place to get us some go-go juice. . . ."

"There ain't nothing out here in the Glades except rattlers, wompus cats, and gators," I pointed out, "but I'll go on ahead and have me a look. . . ." And with that I touched deep six again.

Well, I drove past a lot of fake-out Indian souvenir shops, a drive-in showing X-rated stuff like "THE SWAMP," loads of birds with their skinny legs sticking out of the water, a couple of backpackers, an Indian laundromat, "Washim Dryem," a Stukey Peanut Brittle and a MacShane Hot Potato Chip Stand, and more swamp and mosquito clouds. Then pretty soon, or rather, after a while, I slid to a stop in front of a run-down, tin-roofed gas station with only one pump. And that had an old-fashioned winged red flying horse such as I hadn't seen, even down south, since F.D.R. was President.

The place stank like a big septic tank, and there were mosquitos biting mosquitos it was so buggy. On the porch, festooned by flypaper hangings, sat a lean, stony-faced geezer with a harelip who made no effort to move when I drove up. Except for the squawk of some birds, the place looked like God had abandoned it entirely. The fellow on the porch was rocking himself back and forth for company with his eyes shut.

"Howdy," I said. "You always this busy?"

Fella looked like what I call a Lorna. How do I know? Well, Lornas can never prune their own trees and that geek sure looked like he couldn't and wouldn't, even if you could get him up to try.

"Are you always kept hopping like this?" I asked the man.

"Business?" He grinned. "Hell yes. I had three cars and a motor home in here all the same time last April. Course that was Easter weekend. Always picks up then. People using the cat boxes, don't you know? Bring your own paper, I'm afraid . . ."

A genuine Lorna. He grinned more like a mole than a hare. I said, "That kind of high pressure business can make you crazy, that's for sure."

Nothing.

He'd closed his eyes again and was rocking back and forth fit to be tied.

I said, "This place reminds me of a little roadhouse in Texas. Place called Hamburger Dan . . ."

"Why don't you just cut the shit," the fellow said, "and get on with business? I ain't got all day."

Because there seemed to be only that one pegasus-style pump, I asked if he also had any diesel fuel.

"If I had any more diesel," he said, "I'd have to join OPEC. Let me tell you a little story, young man . . ."

"I'm afraid I'm in a big rush, mister. . . ."

"What's your hurry?" he asked me then. "I got plenty of the stuff here. That's a two ton pump. More than enough to drown a cat. This fella I know says I got enough giggle juice to set some pretty young thing's engine laughing. What do you say to that?"

He rocked furiously once more.

I said, "Excuse me, I'll let you get back to work."

And I headed back toward the CB in my Trans-Am.

"Snowman," I said, "if you get yer ears on, back it down about ten miles ahead at the sign, and then take a left. We got us an oil baron all our own."

"Ten Roger." Snowman was right back at me. "We truckin' as quick as we can. I want to check our passenger when we stop. I ain't heard anything for a while."

A few minutes later I'm diddling the Trans-Am with the gas hose and Snowman rolls up to a stop and climbs out of the cab with Frog and begins to walk toward the pump.

Snowman says, "Ever hear of pusholinc? That's Arkansas for what you got there. Seems this fella down by Fort Smith once built himself a car with the engine in the back and a set of three sleeve valves . . . like the old Jordans . . . *remember them* . . . ?"

"When you leave the canyons of the city," I recited, "your wild hair flying in the wind . . ."

"You're too young to remember that, boy," said the geezer. "Had me a Jordan once with only three doors. The playboy model, with a rumble seat. You should have seen my dust. . . ."

"No kidding," went Cletus.

Just then we heard a great moan coming from the trailer that was like a Sherman tank moving uphill with differential problems. I never heard such a noise like that in all my born days. Cletus and me and Frog rushed to the back and opened up those doors. Charlotte was lying on her side, twitching.

"Poor thing," went Frog. "How you feeling, Charlotte?"

"She looks lousy," I pointed out.

"She'll hear you," Frog said.

We got inside the truck and I took Charlotte's head between my hands and held her close. "What's the matter girl? I think she's got a fever," I pointed out. "We should probably get her to a doctor."

The geezer had come to the back of the truck where we were examining Charlotte and he was going on some more about his old Jordan. The good old days. Stuff of that sort to that effect: "She had a slip clutch and I used to let the ladies fool around with that. From zero to 50 mph on the flat in less than 20 seconds. She was some beauty. The only trouble was those three doors didn't allow for much room for fooling around, if you know what I mean."

"Listen, mister," Frog interrupted then, "we have a sick elephant on our hands and we really do need a doctor."

"An elephant doctor?"

"Whatever's available," she insisted.

I let Frog and Snowman attend to Charlotte and went outside with the old man. Going on and on about his old Jordan: "You know that car cost me only $600 F.O.B. Detroit, and when I sold it to my brother-in-law I got three bills back. Car ran just great, like a crazy horse. The ultimate in luxury at a popular price, they called it. Tomato red she was, with a white fabric roof. The ladies called it my come-a-courting car. I called it 'Bedroom Eyes' because it had these two big brass lanterns and yellow foglights too. . . . Wasn't as fancied up as that thing you got over there," he rattled on, "your Trans-Am, but . . ."

"A doctor," I reminded him, "a doctor . . ."

"Speak of the devil," he said.

Because just then we heard this siren growing louder and louder, as if it was growing out of the very swamps along the side of the road, and down the Tamiami Trail came a little moving speck with a ruby light on top and a big wail that grew louder and louder until, presently, it spotted our station and hydroplaned in. It was this big white ambulance limousine. When the guy in a white coat jumped out and ran over to us, I half expected he would be a crocodile or a manatee, but he was just this paunchy doc in white. He seemed very agitated after he had gotten off the Green Stamp. "Can you tell me how we get to Miami?" he asked. "We've been lost for three hours."

I peered in through the side windows of the ambulance at this guy on a stretcher. "What's wrong with him, Doc?"

"Swamp fever," he says. "From it being *damp* in the *swamp*, if you know what I mean."

"Be that as it may," I said, "but we've also got a patient for you to look at, too."

"I already have a patient," says the doc.

"Be patient, Doc," says Snowman from the back of our truck. "We've got a much bigger problem."

"Not to mention a bigger patient," I added, pointing at the truck. "Remember your hypocrite's oath . . ."

"O that . . ."

I pointed to the back of our semi.

"I don't ordinarily make truck calls," the doc said, "but I'll have a look-see if you really want me to."

He walked with me to the rear of the truck.

"Ah . . . an elephant," he said, when he looked inside. Since he was pretty close to elephant size himself, I said, "Very observant of you, Doc."

Then he asked, "But where's the patient?"

"That is the patient, Doc."

Let's have a look." He climbed aboard.

Then Snowman and Frog and me exchanged a lot of knowing grins and such. "Whichever you say," I called out. "We're here to help as best we can."

Snowman and me slammed the doors shut and slipped the latches and locks into place.

I told Snowman, "Now that we have our medical staff on board, I suggest we haul ass for Texas. Does that make sense?"

"Let's shake a little iron, Bandit," he said. "As we got us some miles to cover."

We scrambled aboard our various vehicles. Then the driver of the ambulance came out of the privy zipping himself up, jumped into the driver's seat, gunned his motor, and took off without even looking in the back of the ambulance where his doors were still swinging half open.

Back on the porch in his rocking chair, the gas station proprietor shook his head. "Had me a second-hand Chrysler Airstream, once. You should have seen the way she took off from neutral to high. Never even had to pass first gear. As a matter of fact, there she is, I think . . ."

He was pointing toward the main road onto which that ambulance had just turned off. A big monster of an alligator was standing in its path, just ambling along like something out of "Deliverance" or "Godzilla's Children." Seeing it there, like a big bumpy log with a gap mouth, the driver nosed his vehicle to a cold stop in the middle of the road.

The gator crossed the highway and headed into the opposite swamp. But when the ambulance started up again, accelerating hard, weight transfer caused the poorly latched rear doors to open. The stretcher, complete with one prone patient under covers, slid out and began to trail the ambulance down the highway like a great big platter of mobile gator chow. Of course, that guy up front didn't know what was happening to his own rear end, and it was only when Snowman and I were pretty sure our gator wasn't coming back that we took off, fast as we could.

Behind us now, of course, but at quite some distance,

was old Buford and Junior. The Sheriff hunched all the way over the wheel, no doubt going on about what he would do to me if he ever caught up, or perhaps it was the scenery he was speaking about. Wasn't much like his part of Texas. Down there when they get a swamp they drain the mess and graze cattle on it. I can just hear him going on about "all these stupid Florida swamp rats," and you name it.

Abruptly we heard their voices on our CB monitors and knew they were coming into range again. A big ten pounder.

Buford was saying, "Thrash my vermin if this ain't the most godforsaken place in the whole world. A gator wouldn't even hang out here, if he didn't have to. Come to think of it, Junior, why don't you move to Florida? You'd fit right in with these dummies."

"Daddy, I ain't never leaving home and that's a promise," said the twirp.

"Boy, don't you threaten your flesh and blood kin like that," Buford said.

That kind of nerd talk had all of us in stitches when suddenly we heard Junior's voice again, a whole octave higher. They'd come upon that stretcher moving down the road at the speed limit, 55 mph.

"Lookit, Daddy, up ahead. It must be some sort of sled."

"One of those damn fool little foreign sports cars," Buford replied. "I'd haul his ass over if I wasn't in such a hurry."

He slowed down to match speed with that stretcher.

"Hey, you seen a black Trans-Am going by here?"

"Help . . . swamp fever," the fella called out.

Buford shouted back, "Don't you know you can catch more than swamp fever in one of those little Jap cars?"

He sped off in pursuit of us again.

On a causeway nearby to a drawbridge we'd pulled all the way over to one side on a big long line to wait for the bridge to be lowered again once all the boat traffic had passed through. We saw Buford's hulk come steaming up to a sudden stop. Scanning his rear view mirror as he fidgeted impatiently, Buford's eyes bulged when he saw my Trans-

Am and Snowman's truck parked nearby. He leaped from his seat and ran toward us, beep-beeping all the while in warning.

"Great balls of fire!" he was shouting. "Lord love a duck."

He tiptoed around another stalled truck and came up behind my car and grabbed me by the sleeve of my red shirt.

"I got you, Bandit! Give up. Surrender, you son of a bitch. Your ass is most certainly under arrest."

"Pardon me, stranger," I said, freezing Buford with my coolest look. "I believe you've got your hand on my arm. Maybe you would also like to remove it before I toss your blubbery hulk off this bridge."

Buford wasn't so easily discouraged. He yapped like a dog with his nose out for a bone. "Stranger, huh? I am Sheriff Buford T. Justice and I hereby apprehend you and your friends under every article of the State of Texas except sodomy, sedition, and child abuse. This here's my deputy, my son," Buford added.

Frog was flirting with the boy like she already had him beguiled. When she heard we were under arrest, she turned to old Buford and said, "A son is a son till he takes a wife, but a daughter is a daughter the rest of your life," and she blew a mock kiss at the boy that even got me feeling kinda jealous.

Huffy, the Sheriff turned back to me. "Come on Bandit, I got you red-handed and you know it. . . ."

"Red-sleeved you mean," said I. "Besides, last time I checked this was Florida, not Texas. That kinda puts you out of your jurisdiction."

I didn't mean to be rough on Buford any more than I had to, but I added, "Why don't you just trot on back to the asylum with the rest of the outpatients?"

The Sheriff's beeper nearly drowned me out. He was truly irate and just a little ridiculous, too. "Bandit, you know perfectly well who I am—and you know perfectly well that true justice knows no limits." His beeper interrupted him again. "I arrest you . . . therefore . . . regardless of wherever we are—beep . . . beep."

It was as if he was on TV and they'd just beeped out all the wrong words, leaving in only the baddies. To cover over his own obscenity, Sheriff Justice continued to go "ooohmmmm oohhmmm,'' but I wasn't having any of this stuff any more. I told him, ''Sheriff, this is a strange game for an adult, but everybody's got to do their own thing.''

The drawbridge had come down again. Buford was kneeling in the street praying into his beeper. Snowman was signaling me to get a move on. We piled into our vehicles and took off across to the other side of the river. When we got there, we just stood still a little and watched that spectacle of human folly in action.

From down on his knees, as if praying, Buford got up and heaved himself into his sedan. He started to move after us, but this truck was still blocking his way. He leaned on his horn, but the trucker wouldn't move. Cursing, he got out again and went up to the cab of the truck. One of our good buddies was inside, of course. Baby Face Turtletaub had a face like a choirboy, and that wasn't all he had.

''All right twit,'' yelled Buford, ''roll this sorry hunk of scrap out of my way. This is a law enforcement matter.''

''Sorry pops,'' said Baby Face, ''but I just can't get my old diesel to fire up.''

''Listen, you little punk,'' Buford announced, ''are you gonna move or am I gonna have to kick a little ass and take names?''

Then Baby Face stepped out of his truck, all six feet seven inches and 275 pounds of him. As he towered over Justice, he reached out and grabbed his Sheriff's badge and, before Buford's very own eyes, rolled it and mashed it all together with his hand into a little gold ball which now dangled off his shirt front like a wilted peony flower.

Justice glanced apprehensively at the gold twist on his chest which had once symbolized his authority. ''Heh, heh,'' he was stammering, ''I sure am glad you enjoyed my little attempt at humor. And now *sir*, could I offer my radio for you to call for help?''

''Bullsheeit,'' growled Baby Face. He climbed back into his truck, fired up, and sped off over the bridge.

Justice stood in shock for a moment, and then recovered and sprinted back to his own car. He leaped in and started up the engines.

"Fasten your belt, Junior. We are undertaking full pursuit."

But in his hurry to get going again, Justice failed to notice the red warning light on the bridge was blinking and bells were ringing in his ears even louder than his beeper. As he sped along, that bridge started rising again.

Junior warned him, but Justice said, "Hold on and I'll show you some real driving."

Buford's car reached the gap in the bridge just at the moment when the spans were opening up. The car almost got across, but got hung up between with its bumpers clinging to either edge. Buford jammed it into reverse, then back to drive. The engine revved, the wheels spun, and he was stuck there. Then he ordered Junior to get out and give him a push. The twirp stepped outside, pivoted in the air, and nose-dived straight down maybe 30 feet into the water.

In the nearby booth of the bridge operator, the grizzled old hand who moved the lever was chewing tobacco and reading an *Enquirer*. Looking up, he saw Buford caught between spans. He reached into his pockets and found a quarter and gave it a flip: heads or tails.

When it landed, he pushed the lever to up. That bridge started rising higher and higher. Buford's car was dangling like a button on a shirt front. Its wheels spun, then it lost its grip and fell with a big hard splash down into the river.

VIII

In the Boonies

In the good old days when Frog and I were an item, she used to give me such looks and sweet talk it would damn near pop my buttons. Just one look or a word was often enough. In Vegas, once, she called me "darling," and I was ready to go. But sometimes even "doll boy" was enough. I called her lots of things, too: My Frog, of course, My Heart, My Soul, Little Toad, and Fly. Don't ask me why.

Frog has such pretty hands. She used to pass them through my sidehairs. I loved it when she sat with them on her lap while I was driving. Always so well manicured and trim. A neat, pretty woman with heart, I'd say.

She told me once, "I am your woman now but times could certainly change."

Well change they did, of course, and then we were on the outs, and then we were together again. What can I tell you? After Buford went over the bridge, she came and sat with me in the Trans-Am. I even let her drive for a while to get the feel of the wheel, but nothing much was happening between us you need to worry about.

Then I took over and things began to change a bit. Takes a man to know when to turn and when to hit what pedals.

We were up near Pepsicola somewhere in the Panhandle

when I started clutching. She was doing her lips with pomade and there was nothing but lizards crawling down the road behind us.

I said, "You know, Frog, getting back behind the wheel again, ditching a few smokies, and staying sober as a judge, I am starting to feel right good about myself."

"That's wonderful," she told me. "Let's hope you're not the only one."

I checked out the rear view mirror and saw only Snowman's grinning face and Fred licking his chops next to him.

"What's not to love," I asked, "I mean?"

"When you're a little better," she said, with a wry little grin, "I'll tell you."

Then she started to sing, an old hit song from the radio:

"Compassion
It's the thing we do together.
Compassion
In foul or stormy weather.
It's the thing we do
Together
On the grass
Or in the heather.
Don't knock it.
It's our thing . . ."

"Nice song," I said.

"My friend Charmayne bought me the record," said Frog. " 'The Bullies.' "

"How is Charmayne?" I asked.

"She's still chasing that Billy Jack Bulip," said Frog, "and getting nowhere fast."

She started to giggle a laugh, and then checked herself and turned glum. Wasn't giving me no more bright ideas. "We'll cross over into Alabama any minute," she said. "It's morning already and we've been running all night long. Don't you think we ought to stop and see what the doc has to say?"

"If you say so, honey love, sure." I picked up the CB mike. "Snowman, what's shaking with Charlotte?"

"Ain't heard a thing," he told me. "Don't suppose the Doc got squashed, do you?"

I opined as how it just might be and that we better have us another look-see. We rolled to the side of the road near an old brown patch of spartina grass and got out and walked to the rear of the trailer. Overhead a Tupelo swallow chortled raucously down at us.

After we got the back doors open, Frog asked, "How is she, Doc?"

"Can't tell," he said, agreeably enough. "I'll have to get her off the truck just to examine her properly. . . . Where are we?"

"Not too far from Mobile," Snowman softly explained, "and on our way to Texas."

The doctor was pretty upset about that piece of news. "I have patients in Miami I'm worried about. . . ."

Charlotte moaned again, and I said, "Don't worry about them, they'll be fine."

"You think so."

"Sure," I said. "Now about this elephant."

She was lying on her side, her big round face and wrinkly trunk a mask of pitiful and profound woe. Again she moaned, setting my bowels a-throb.

The doc said again, "I must get her off this truck if I am to give her a more thorough examination."

We'd wasted a whole lot of precious time in Miami getting Charlotte out of her crate so I said, "Why can't you examine her while we drive? We're losing a lot of time . . ."

Cletus wouldn't let me finish my sentence. He wouldn't hear of such a thing. "The elephant's health comes first. . . ."

"Maybe it's just a bad case of *elephantiasis*," I said, trying to make a joke of it to lighten all our moods, but Frog became reproachful. "Some animal lover you are. . . . Can't you take your cues from Snowman?"

My good buddy leaned over close to me and pointed out as to how if there was no elephant there'd be no pesos.

Well even I could respect logic like that, so I came right up close to Charlotte and started petting her again. "You're gonna be alright, girl. I'm here for you, Bandit Pandit. . . ."

The doc became instantly bossy. "Take her over to that patch of sassafras grass, and set her down on her side."

We tried to do as we were told.

As we moved off, I heard the doc muttering, "Now where did I put that big tongue depressor . . . and my hot water bottle? . . . I could fill it from a radiator, I suppose. . . ."

Problem was, Charlotte was restless. It took two of us to hold her down, one by the ears and the other by her hind legs. She lay there panting, all swollen and puffy, like a great big sow with an extra leg and a nozzle at the end of it. And all the while she moaned and grunted and nuzzled me whenever I came too near to her. As the song says, compassion is the thing we do together.

As Charlotte's breathing eased, I whispered every kindness I could think of into her big fan-like ears, and then the doc came over and had her open wide.

Abruptly Frog commenced to sing the second stanza of that Bullies hit:

> *"Even elephants need compassion.*
> *Great or small, it's all the fashion.*
> *Let's be sweet to one another.*
> *Otherwise why should we bother?*
> *It's the thing we do together*
> *Puts us in a special lather*
> *Give me love, or give me . . ."*

"Frog," I said, "better let this poor thing relax. Don't confuse her with so much foolish stuff."

"It's alright," the doc says, "she seems to like to be sung to. She's opening up. Lookit. Now say 'ahhh' . . ."

> *"Even chipmunks need compassion,*
> *Small or great, or doggy fashion . . ."*

Out there in a patch of sassafras grass by the side of the road near Pepsicola, too.

Meanwhile, after getting fished out of the river, Buford and Junior were once again in drenching hot pursuit of us.

They must have been burning as much water as oil, because we could hear them on our CB monitors again, even though they were still miles away. It sure sounded as though they were both gargling.

Reminds me a lot of my Uncle Val first time he went visiting his wife's rich relatives down there in Palm Beach, Florida. Val comes out of the airport lounge with his suitcase and he decided to go across this sorghum field to his rental car and falls right into an old cesspool. Up to his neck in the you-know-what and he's calling out, "FIRE FIRE FIRE HELP FIRE!" Well his wife is standing by and she calls the Fire Department and they eventually come and fish him out with a big net.

Well then she asks Val, "How come you were yelling fire anyway, Val?"

"Who can say shit in Palm Beach, Florida?" replies he.

Likewise with Buford and Junior. They was just balling the jack as best they could, but their exhaust pipe was blowing water bubbles out the rear end, and down near the other side of Pepsi, over to the Naval Airbase, they rounded a corner and come upon a police car with its lights flashing. They were real gung ho for trouble when they saw these three dudes hassling with each other: two whites and a black guy. You copy?

Well the black dude has an arm around one of the white guys by the neck, and he's trying to hoist up a hammer lock on the other. Buford Justice thought "lawmen in trouble," and he leaped out of his car and forced the black dude to release the boy in the hammer lock, who immediately took off.

Watching him leave, or so I was told, Buford immediately drew on the black man and told the other white, "Way to go, Sheriff. You get the rest of the gang and I'll hold this one until you're back . . ."

"Where did you come from?" the black dude asked then, still struggling with the other pale dude.

So Buford says, "Texarkana, Texas . . . to the rescue, as it were, *lickety-split* . . ."

He broke the black dude's grip and helped the other

white guy to get free and take off, and then he threw a bear hug around the black guy and held him like that. Real tight like that.

"*You may be in deep trouble, Texarkana,*" says the guy who's black. He happened to be dressed all in black, too, and when Buford told Junior to put the cuffs on him, the little twirp stepped out of his car and saw a big gold sheriff's badge on the front of his black tunic.

"Daddy," he said, "I'll hold him and you put the cuffs on him . . ."

"Everything I have to do myself," went Buford. But as soon as he walked around in front of his prisoner his beeper started up galore, and he had to drop down into his ritual position and start in with all those "ooohms" all over again.

Some folks never learn, I guess, or change that much. They don't know compassion from an old coon joke. Fellers like Buford, though, they really got no excuses. Where their brains are the Almighty put something else: a mess of bad habits and traditions. No place in the new South for stuff like that. Give me brotherhood and compassion any day in the week. The rest, as they say, sucks like wet moccasins.

But the fact was, there are times which try the souls of even the best of men, such as me, Bandit. The doc was taking his sweet time with that eye, ear, nose, and throat exam, and after a while it became downwright unendurable hanging around with Frog and not being able to even flirt just a little bit with her. I paced back and forth with my hands in my jeans, and then I finally invited Carrie to take a little stroll with me in the woods while we was waiting. I had some things to talk over.

To my surprise she even agreed.

"Give a call,"I told Snowman.

"Be good, kids," he grinned.

We went out toward a tiny copse where there was a patch of scrubby piney woods, and beyond that was some bigger pines in which the State had built a sort of camping area with picnic tables, fireplaces, and comfort stations.

A bunch of my fellow truckers had pulled in there from the access road, and they was barbecuing and raising a little hell. When they saw me with my own favorite little piece of barbecue, they all started whistling and greeting me with hellos, and what-have-yous. Feller named Don Williams even asked, "What are you cooking up for us this time, Bandit?"

"Don't talk fresh," I said. "This one's a lady. . . ."

"I meant, what are you running?" he demanded.

"*Machs nix*," I replied. I stopped to look him over, because I knew him from the old days. He sure as hell was all beat up, bruised, and generally in what I would call very rough shape.

Since he was such a young feller, I asked, "Son, I want you to tell me who did that to you."

"*Aw* Bandit," he said, turning mawky, "I don't want you jumping into the skillet over me."

"I want to know so I'll stay clear of him," I said. "Just tell me what happened."

"If the lady wasn't here, I would," Don said.

Frog said, "I can take a hint," and gave me a faint little toodle-oo wave with her hand and strolled off toward a nearby lily pond.

Then Don said, "Me and my buddy Bill here, we made up a little song about what happened. Why don't you just grab yourself a rib and dip it in some sauce and we'll sing it to you?"

Then he picked up his guitar and began to sing:

"*Supply side economics*
and I'm on the go again
Making other mens' profits
Standing out in the rain . . ."

"Sounds like a trucker's lament," I said when he was through. "Still, I don't understand what happened. How about more story and less argument?"

I was watching Frog, sitting by her lily pond, pluck a certain daisy and trim off the petals one by one. *He loves me . . . He loves himself*, which is what she always said at such moments: loves me, loves *him* . . .

Pronto, Don started in a-strumming again:

* * *

"Once in Wounded Knee, Dakota
Stopped to have an Indian soda
Smokies everywhere a-shooting
Served me blood with sarspa putum."

"*Sarspa putum?*" I asked. "What in hell is that?"

"Just needed a rhyme word for sarsparilla," said Don.

But I really don't like politics and poetry when they're so mixed up together like that in a song, and I said, "Another time fellas. *Right on.*" I wandered over to where my Frog was sitting, crumpling up the rest of her daisy, like a White Rock ad, only with her clothing on.

"*Hi, Darlin . . .*"

"*Hi . . .*"

In the background, Don strummed loud and soft:

"Took my mother to the barber
Near the Brownsville Texas harbor
Oily waters in the Gulf
Oily shrimps are half a loaf . . ."

Then his buddy chimed in:

"Capitalism makes men greedy,
Be a Wobbly, serve the needy . . ."

"My sentiments exactly," said Carrie, ever the feminist.

"*Aw darlin' . . .*"

"*What?*" I'd picked up a little something at a store during our last rest stop and I had it held in my hands behind my back.

I pulled it out now, all gift-wrapped fancy like it was Christmas or Valentine's Day: "*For you*, dar . . ."

"How sweet, Bandit."

She tore open the wrappers and there was a little 45 rpm of my one and only record. "The Semi Drag" was on one side and on the flip was "Doing The 18 Wheel Hop."

"We only cut 700 of them," I pointed out.

"Yeah," she said, slightly disappointed, "and I think I

saw just about all of them at a couple of K-Marts we passed recently. They were giving it away with Moksi cola. . . ."

Don Williams sang on and on:

> "*Whoever said we should hop into bed*
> *Got a hole in his head*
> *Which you also gave me* once . . ."

"Nice song," Frog frowned. "Pleasing sentiments. You know I did a little work in the music business."

"You did?" No reason why I shouldn't play her straight man for a change. Never can tell what I might get in return.

She mumbled, "Uh . . . huh . . . I actually managed a group called 'The Scabs'. . . ."

"*How did you ever manage to get them?*"

I laughed at my own joke, but Carrie did me one better: "It was in New York at the movie *Norma Rae*. All the ushers were feeling wobbly. There was a strike. And they refused . . ."

"Bloody fools," I said.

"Very funny," Frog said. "Really, it's too bad nobody ever heard of them, because I was a great manager, but one thing I couldn't even manage to do was get them a job."

She looked a little sad and discouraged again, and that was surely something to think about. Which is what we both did, then, as those pond frogs croaked, and the crickets did their thing, too, and the chiggers bit each other, and Don Williams strummed on and on, and on again.

Suddenly we heard Snowman shouting: "Bandit . . . Frog . . . come here, come quick . . . Charlotte's in trouble . . ."

Frog was off and running already and I had to grab her and hold her back to get in even another word with her.

"Sometimes I think you like that elephant better than me. . . ."

"JUST HOLD THAT THOUGHT," she said.

She shrugged loose and took off.

I stood there for a minute listening to the glissando sounds of nature and Don Williams: "*Give me the moon over Mussel Shoals . . . and I'll give you a nuclear tomorrow . . .*"

I told myself then, "Am I losing it?" Then I looked myself over in the mirror of that pond real careful. "Naahh."

When I took off after Carrie I was humming "Ozark Fraulein."

IX

Great Expectations

I caught up with Frog again at the near lip of the sassafras patch; Doc and Snowman were just washing their hands in radiator water, after having finished their examination. Doc sure looked kind of elated, but Snowman seemed a little worried.

Frog ran over to them, breaking tall reeds as she stepped. "What's wrong with Charlotte? She's alright?"

"I'll say," said the Doc. "She's just fine. Now let's hope the baby is as healthy."

I could just about hear the word "baby" and saw the look of glee on Frog's pretty face.

"*Baby?*" I demanded. "*Did I hear baby?*"

"He said it," went Snowman.

"Why did he say baby?" I turned to the doc himself. "Why did you say baby?"

"Because that big girl's pregnant. Knocked up . . ."

"Pregnant?" I asked. "Who did it?"

"Don't you look at me," went Snowman.

"Naturally," said the doc, "it would be a breach of professional confidence for me to go into too many of the details, but I think it's safe to say Charlotte conceived many months ago. It appears she'll give birth any day."

"*So what are we going to do now?*" I asked, just for my own curiosity, but it came out sorta sounding like I was truly perplexed and that's what Snowman, at least, responded to.

"I'll tell you what we're gonna do," he said. "We're gonna keep an eye out for the biggest goddamn stork you ever saw."

"Don't be so funny, Snowman," I said, ever cooperative. "We're not going to let a little pregnancy stop our forward motion."

"Never did before," he opined, spitting out a quid in the direction of Mobile.

I hot chigger-footed right over to Charlotte and tugged her up by the rope. "Okay sweetheart, you've had your fun. Now we're going."

A regular White 20-wheeler I had at the end of that rope. Jumbo in spades.

"Somebody kindly help me move this mother," I called out.

Frog rushed over with a look of obstinate care and took the rope out of my hand, but not to help me, I'm afraid.

"Bandit," she said, "we're not moving Charlotte anywhere."

That's like saying how I might like to walk barefoot over hot coals. I stomped my foot like Rumpelstiltskin and said, "We have to get to Dallas and pretty quick."

"No!"

"It will be better for Charlotte, too," I said. "Dallas happens to be world-renowned for its excellent elephant medical care. The so-called Mammoth Medical Center . . ."

"Cut it out with the jokes," she said. "Let's ask the doc what he thinks." She came toward him with a look of earnest petition. "Should we move her Doc?"

I had to admit I was waving a fistful of money behind her back while she spoke to him, but doc was an honest man and couldn't be bought.

"I've seen births take place in some very odd places. Once I even delivered a baby elephant aboard a submerged submarine and with nothing but ordinary kitchen utensils . . . *but*," he added, "despite all that, and the fact that she is evidently robust and among her loved ones, I don't think

Charlotte should be traveling anywhere. At least not without a good night's rest."

"We can't afford a single night, goddamnit," I said. "I'm putting my foot down."

Snowman soothed me. "If she was my old woman, in her condition, I know just how I'd be feeling. . . ."

But as he soon saw sentiments wouldn't sway me, he was cool and practical again. "Lookit Bandit buddy, I want the money as much as you do, but we sure ain't gonna get diddly by delivering a dead elephant."

"Softy . . . You . . . You get soft like that," I said, "and the South will never rise again, much less you. . . . Now," I added, "we're not staying the night and that's that . . ."

I went over to Charlotte again and grabbed her rope as though to tug her up on her knees. So determined was I, I probably could have hauled Mount St. Helens over to meet Mr. Mohammed. It was real sweaty hard work and at first I wasn't getting nowhere. Crickets chattered at my efforts; the twilight was coming on, and with it clouds of thorny little gnats. From far away I could hear the voice of Don Williams: "*Adios Pretty Ozark Fraulein* . . ."

I put my shoulder to that rope and just yanked. But nothing happened. A piece about a foot long even came loose in my hand. Frog must have cut it there. But now she sidled up to me, real seductive-like. "Too bad Bandit, but don't let this spoil our good time. I've kind of missed you all these months and it's hard to get reacquainted at 110 mph. Would it be so bad to spend one night under the stars . . . together. . . ?"

Well I guess, in the long run, some arguments are just more convincing than others. I put my arm around Frog and said, "Good night everybody, see you in the morning."

We had drifted off from that lying-in scene in a sort of erotic fog, with me holding Carrie by the hand and nuzzling sweet nothings into her neck, headed for the nearby woods. But when I nuzzled her it was Charlotte, not Frog, who moaned back.

Strange response.

When I stopped, Charlotte stopped moaning.

It's as if those two ladies were wired together somehow. Still Frog asked, "What's wrong with *her*?"

"I don't know. Let's go," I said, "you know . . . get reacquainted . . ."

I pulled her toward those woods again with another little nuzzle, but Charlotte moaned right back even louder.

Stopped in our tracks, we watched as Charlotte staggered up to her feet and came between Frog and me with her trunk, an act of total irate jealousy.

Snowman was hooting like a coyote with a bellyful of jumping beans. "*Hee heee*, she's in love is all, Bandit. With you. . . . The big ones always did go for you."

"Cletus ain't just whistling," Carrie says. "She really seems jealous of me. . . . Back off Charlotte," she added, again, joking.

And the doc pointed out that jealousy may become a green-eyed monster, but "pregnant women have all kinds of crazy emotions at such times."

"Must be like what you feel if you eat too much seafood or sweets," he concluded.

"So do all of us horny daredevils," I replied, testily. I grabbed Frog and started pulling on her, but Charlotte stomped and snorted and moaned. She was fit to be tied and threatened to run amuck. She was having the vapors, trumpeting away like a dying swan and butting at me with her head.

The less things change the more they remain the same, they always say in my part of Texas, and I guess that's just what Carrie had in mind when she turned to me so sweetly then. "She really shouldn't let herself get upset at a time like this . . ."

She ran her lovely fingers through my hair, patted my flanks, made little spitcurl knots, and breathed the warmth of her entire sweet body onto mine.

Ah sweet mystery of life . . .

When she told me, "Sometimes we all have to make sacrifices," I was in such entire agreement that I gladly accepted my fate as Charlotte's paramour.

The things a man will do for a woman. That night we all slept out: Doc, Snowman, Fred, and Frog in one bunch; and a little distance off, Charlotte and me, with her trunk slung across my shoulders like a Hawaiian pun. So tight and close together were we that when I tried to draw away Charlotte drew me even closer with her trunk.

Needless to say, the pleasure was all hers and a moaning sleepless night was mostly all mine.

X

The Slammer for Buford and Other Such Matters

How my daddy came by his name is an amusing story to recount. His full name was Honus Wagner Bandit, because his own pappy and mammy happened to be North Carolina baseball fans and went to all the games down in the Piedmont League. Now grandma, she'd been married before, to a sailor; and when he shipped out and never did come back, she vowed she'd be sober as a nun the rest of her life.

Well, so then she met my grandpa Zed at a baseball park, and he courted her good and plenty. After they finally fell in love she told her sister, "Husband number one couldn't hold a bat to what my darling Zed was all about." So when their first baby was born she named the boy in his honor, naturally, as the superstar of his day, Honus Wagner.

Frog once told me she almost became a superstar nun once, on the TV, until she broke the habit; and it's a good thing she didn't, I've always said. And I guess you should know I was named after that comedian from the Texaco Hour, Mr. Milton Berle. Only they reversed it to make it more Southern: my name being Burl Milton.

But I'm mentioning all these examples of human oddity and folly because I want to say it's my honest opinion nobody has to go looking to be stupid. We just are sometimes, is all.

The only person I ever knew who went deliberately out of his way to make a jackass out of himself, coming and going, was Sheriff Buford T. Justice. That one—you could blindfold him and bend him over backwards, and he wouldn't be able to figure out how to stand up straight again. When they was giving out brains he volunteered for kitchen police.

Blacks may be used to dealing with dummy lawmen like that; I'm not. When Buford was arrested by that black sheriff for interfering with "a lawful arrest of two alleged perpetrators," the only expression I had for him was "hell deserving old rascal."

Poor old Buford, he was so scared his pupils were sticking out like two buckeyes flung against a mud wall. He looked just like a cockroach in a hot skillet. The sheriff wanted to put him right into the slammer, but after checking down in Texarkana on the radio he agreed to let Buford go along his merry way, pending a hearing.

Standing in the gathering dusk and gloaming while he awaited receipt of his summons, Buford must have looked like he was about to come out of his own britches. I imagine him saying some dumb thing like, "My word. The sun will never set on me in this town again."

"Frankly I can't wait," says the sheriff, "to hear you tell Judge Crickback how those two escaped."

Then he turns to Junior with his gentle smile. "It's a shame one can't pick their own parents. I am sure you could have done better."

Buford's beeper was doing S.O.S. as that sheriff ambled back to his own squad car and Junior replied, "I agree with that nice man, Daddy."

So then Buford's beeper goes real crazy. He's fuming, downright irate. As if he'd been bit by some rabid dog or cat.

"I knew," he said, "this would happen once we gave them bussing."

As I say, you teach an old dog like Buford new tricks and it turns out he still ain't housebroken.

So he and Junior went on their way again, considerably chastised, but not so personally as he was going to lay off. The man ain't born as persistently dumb as him. They must have driven all night long without sleep, because next morning when we got back on the road making pretty good time we could hear them faint as ghosts in our CB monitors.

Great balls of fire. Frog was back in the Trans-Am with me, and Snowman and Fred in the truck, with the doc attending to Charlotte. We were making real good time. Speedwise, that is . . .

Every once in a while I'd hear Snowman gabbing at us across the ether: "Ain't seen a Smokey for hours. A-O.K. between here and Louisiana . . ."

"Knock on wood," I'd reply, doffing my hat and offering the top of my head to Frog. "Knock on wood, babe."

Then outside Oyster Point it rained a little, big beads of wet grimy water, tainted from the nearby petro-crackers even as they mixed with the wet air. We slowed down to see better. The Snowman related as how he was going to spend his share of the swag. He said, "Gwine to get my wife and kids something they always wanted . . . a holiday trip to Hawaii . . . and Waikiki . . ."

"That's sure sweet, Snowman," said Frog. "You sure must love your family."

"*Hell,*" he laughed, "I ain't *gwine* with them!"

Laughing at him, I hollered back, "What in hell is that *gwine* business, Cletus?"

And Carrie she declared as how "Snowman sure wasn't much of a family man."

So I explained for her he sure was. "Everytime he manages an overnighter sleep-over date at his house, his family increases . . ."

Snowman was singing his explanation: "*Gwine* to set my heart at ease . . . *Gwine* to take a sentimental journey . . ." and Fred was barking something fit to scare chickens and I turned him down low.

"You know," I told her then, "been thinking a lot about having a kid myself someday . . . a little girl."

Frog took me in with her glance of amorous curiosity. "Why not a little boy?"

"Well, to put a handle on it," I said, "I'm worried if I have a son, he'd turn out just like me."

"That wouldn't be so bad," she smirked.

"*Bad?*" She wasn't getting the big picture. "He'd be

magnificent. . . . A young hotshot like that would cut in on my action. That's the rumor,'' I pointed out. ''So-called talk of the town in effect . . . words to that . . . so on . . . so forth . . .'' Petering out, my voice was trailing off. I admired myself in the rear view mirror and there was Buford's scowl, pulling up in his battered sedan to within an RCH of our Trans-Am.

Over the CB, Buford keened at me ominously through patches of glare static: ''Hello . . . sommmamabitch! Cuzzy bastard, I'm coming to get your sommammmma . . . GLACK,'' and there was the high steady ear-piercing blare of feedback from our cars being jammed so close together.

I grabbed the mike. ''Snowman, you keep on slow boatin' and I am really gonna shake some trees. We got our favorite Countie Mountie on our donkey. Copy me?''

''Me and Fred will carry it on, son.''

I pulled around Cletus' truck and scooted off into the dust with Buford in hot pursuit. They say a man is only as good as his tires. I took every turn on the crusty edge of my treads, broke fierce hot gusts of wind through my twin pipes when I geared up, jammed on my jammers only to slow me down to 90 mph, and felt the air against my face like a soothing lotion. Ripping asphalt with Frog as Buford tried to keep within spitting distance was a trip to the other side of a dream.

Once, in a small town's main drag, to steer clear of an old boy on the dodder, I made a quick right and then hung a left again and slid in through a gate marked ''Swamp County Fairground.'' Those fairgrounds were deserted, a ''closed'' sign peeling off the gate. Buford hung tight on my tail as we tucked another left around a comfort station and then skidded past a maintenance man on his tractor.

''Hey you guys,'' the tractor driver pointed out, ''fair ain't open again until next spring.''

All around the mulberry bush we went, as I struggled mightily with the swinging wheel, twitching it full lock in both directions. I didn't even stop to look down at the results. My foot was touching China under the floorboards.

Buford was driving about as hard, too, but not nearly as well as me. There was one of these huge wooden roller coasters sprouting from the fairground, and as we spun in and under its wooden girders and struts, he kept clouting against them, tearing off splintery chunks of wood and bits of fender. Buffeting he was, in the front seat, like a cat on the electric chair when they hit the juice.

Over the CB I heard him silencing Junior's protests: "Shut up and watch how I do this. Some day you may have to fill my shoes."

I have a hunch poor Junior's shoes were already filling up—with you know what.

All I had to look at behind me in the rear view mirror was Buford's mighty and determined scowl. As I powered out from under another loop of the roller coaster, I saw a gap in the fence, leaned all the way back on two wheels and, singing "Ozark Fraulein" all the while, leaped across to the other side of the road.

Frog was reaching for digitalis, and my hairpiece almost came unstuck, but we made it for sure. And when Buford tried the same stunt, he climbed a piece of wall, blew a tire, and fell down hard again on his chassis and underpinnings, skidding to a stop.

Buford was pounding at his steering wheel. He should have disconnected his beeper too. From across the way I hummed while listening to the CB monitor as Junior tried to comfort him.

"You did real good, Daddy, only hitting 42 of those two-by-four support braces. . . ."

"You think I'm some kind of dummy or something?" asked the sheriff.

"*Fraulein Fraulein,*" I was singing, until I heard a sound like wood splintering commence. Then I saw the heads of Buford and Junior both turn as that gigantic wooden roller coaster tumbled all the way over and disintegrated piece by piece in one huge massive and spectacular collapse. Huge balls of dust and sawdust splinters rose from the crash of that immense wooden erection, and the noise was like a big road blast through rock. Birds scattered for miles; the lizards scampered.

As if anticipating the abrupt decline and fall of the roller coaster by maybe half a minute, Old Buford had his head between his legs, his hands on his head, beeper signaling at Martians. Junior was crossing himself, too, world without end amen.

Then a man sprinted up to their car looking rather angry and stuttered at them, "Uh, sir, I uh, am th—the owner of thi—this roller coaster, and I have a couple of . . . que–questions. . . ."

Coming out of hiding, Buford asked, "Spit it out boy, we ain't got all day. A hardened criminal is on the loose . . ."

"I am wondering who is going to pay for all this damage," says the stutterer.

"Sheriff's Department of Texarkana, Texas," says Buford. "That's who. Just make out a bill marked *O-fishel* Business . . ."

"Alright, *fishel*," says the man, "I'll be right back with my pad and pencil."

XI

Laboring

Down through Alabama and Louisiana the road we took dilated and contracted like a writhing snake. Couldn't make much worse time than we did in places, and at other points it opened wide like a horn of plenty and we just roared our way along.

Swamp country and piney woods alternated, but there are parts of the South, even down there, which are more like Texas than magnolia country. Once we stopped in such a place, in cattle country near the town of La Mays, to give Charlotte a little exercise.

Figuring we had such a good lead on Buford, we all just took a rest on the grass while Doc gentled Charlotte around in circles on a lead rope. That was so dizzying it was difficult at times to tell who was who.

Frog and I were just holding hands a little, sort of sweet and gentle then, when Snowman came over with a worried look on his face.

I saw there was a problem right away and asked, "What's up?"

Snowman said, "Ask the doc."

I got up and brushed myself down and walked over to

where he and the elephant and Doc were doing their little promenade. "Problems, Doc?"

"Charlotte can't go on," he said with professional care. "I think she must be starting to have her pains."

"Her pains?"

"Labor, Bandit," said Froggy, joining up with us. "I think we've got to get her off her feet, and plenty of hot water, and towels . . . no?"

"Just off her feet will do for the moment," said the doc. "That's definitely the issue. She's carrying too much weight on her and it's too bouncy in there for her to lie on her stomach."

I was in such a state I wasn't hearing any of it. "Maybe she's just looking for a little attention."

"O Bandit," Frog said.

Charlotte glared at me like a crossed lover, gave another deep sigh and moan, and slid down to a sitting position. She wouldn't move no matter how hard I pulled at her rope. Damn beast, she was almost human. Finally I grabbed her trunk, but she made us look like a bad dog act the way she moaned and groaned and lay her head down and closed her eyes.

Then the doc came up, and gently pried open one eye, and peered inside.

"A little Demerol will help . . . for the pains," he said, "but not too much or she'll go under, and we don't want that." He peered at me again, like I was also his patient. "Listen, Mr. Bandit, you know your business and I know mine. I don't think she can go on."

"We gotta finish this job. I need the money. I need it." It was agitating to contemplate such a delay. I slapped my thigh, and it was almost numb, as if I was in some kind of horrible twilight sleep.

Snowman lay a hand on my shoulder. "Afraid that's it, good buddy. That's all she ever wrote for us, Lady Luck. We sure gave it a hell of a shot."

"It can't be," I protested. "We've just got to . . ."

"Why don't you do the right thing just once in your life?" Frog reproached me.

Well, I was barely listening. I sure didn't want any

further breach to develop between Carrie and me. I kept looking at poor suffering Charlotte, too, and finally I was moved a little to tears of pity and compassion, just like in the old song.

"How much rest will she need, Doc?" I inquired.

"A few hours, at very least," he explained.

"Hey, sweet buddy," Snowman said, "let's take our minds off of our troubles. We'll beeline it to Mobile or Biloxi for a spat of wine, women, and song."

"What do you think, honey?" I asked Frog.

"Well," she said, "I really don't want any women, but it's fine otherwise. . . ."

"Wine and song for Frog," said Snowman. "Easy on the women. Let's go."

The two of them took me by the hand and led me off to the Trans-Am. I went along, of course, but my mind was elsewhere worrying and fretting. It was as if I'd probably even have to labor just to have me a good time. I had Frog ask the doc if he would also like to join our party.

"I'll stay with my patient," he said. Marcus Fatboy, M.D.

It turned out Sheriff Buford had ten feet of damages and charges to be read off to him by that stuttering roller coaster owner, such as the replacement cost of 6,000 150-watt light bulbs, for example, and Justice couldn't get on his way till it was all read off to him and signed for. So he was a passel delayed in giving chase to us once again, and by then we had, indeed, backtracked all the way to Mobile, which we were now 50 miles beyond, and there was still no sight or sound of him and his kin.

By the time we got to Mobile, in fact, I was in a mite cheerier mood, remembering that time the mayor gave me the keys to the city at the Municipal Auditorium. Well, this time we went to the Elephant's Castle, a chic new downtown multi-racial disco with New Wave sounds. The place was really jumping.

Sweet jive alive, it was jumping like a dog with fleas. Frog and I sat out a lot of the dancing at a ringside table, but Snowman went right off into deep water with two foxes, one black and one white, in the middle of the floor.

THE ADVENTURES OF
SMOKEY AND THE BANDIT
BANDIT

That's suave me,
Burl Milton Bandit—
lookin' like Burt Reynolds—
behind the wheel of
my Trans Am.

Sheriff Buford T. Justice and me, calmly engaged in a most profound and enlightenin' discussion.

Talk about crunchin' metal, Buford and his car went head-on with that eighteen-wheeler and got flattened.

My ole buddy Snowman, his good ole hound dog Fred, and me, gettin' ready to hightail it out of the Sheriff's clutches.

Ain't anyone safe from that
crazy drivin' Sheriff?

Who else but Buford could convert
his car into a convertible so unexpectedly.

A battered Buford and his son Junior on the lookout for Carrie, that beautiful runaway bride.

This ain't no steeplechase, just Carrie flyin' in my Trans Am and takin' on those hurdles.

It's me and Frog, that fast-talkin'
runaway beauty who claims she used to be a flyin' nun.

Nope. It's not a victory sign.
I'm just orderin' up a couple of cans of cold beer
so's me and my buddy can start the day fresh.

When chasin' me, Sheriff Buford T. Justice sometimes
finds out that the shortest distance between
two points can lead to disaster of titanic proportions.

MOUNTED
POLICE

Whatta beautiful sight! A good ole-fashioned higgledy-piggledy. It's pile-up time at the O.K. car crunch corral. Ya'd think that the Smokies would have learned by now that ya don't mess with Bandit.

Smokies hot on my trail, hot under the collar.

Me and Frog, awaitin' to find out what new plot ole Buford has hatched.

What do ya do when a ten-foot pregnant elephant has the hots for ya and wants to show affection?

Me and Frog in the Trans Am, pedal to the metal, headin' it into the sunset—hightailin' that machine up and over the roadblock set up by a gang of Smokies. Over and out.

He was drinking French 75s—champagne and brandy fizzed together. We were sipping big pink sloe gins. Frog was bouncing in her seat to the music, but, as I say, I had turned more than just a little thoughtful. I was totally preoccupied, doodling away on a cocktail paper napkin and drawing a nice little house with a yard in front and back, a couple of cars in the garage, and kids inside a playpen.

The things your mind will do sometimes. A couple of people walked up to our table and gave me the high sign, but I was not into socializing either. All that loud disco noise made me all the quieter, even as it seemed to excite Frog more and more.

"Listen to that music, bubbah, doesn't it get you off? Come on honey," she urged, "let's dance."

Let's dance, let's dance. That sounded more like old Glen Miller than what we were getting blistered by at ringside: "GOTTA HAUNCH OF WOMAN AND SHE MAKE ME CRY . . ."

Nevertheless, I watched Carrie dance her way down the aisle out of range of my table.

"She sure is a cute little twitcher," said Snowman, leaning over me, all in a sweat.

My mind was a million miles away. That was the only way I could duck all that noise, while I calculated whether I could just figure a way to get her off her feet.

Seeing my mind at work like that (and the drawing I'd just made on the cocktail napkin resembling a double bed), Snowman told me, "Hell, just get her drunk and turn the lights off."

"I'm not talking about Frog," I said. "I'm talking about Charlotte." And I guess I really was, after all, despite all the domestic fantasies, because it was right about then that I saw the light. My brainstorm was a whole goddamn apparatus. I started doodling again, fast and furious.

Frog urged, "Come on, Bandit, let's do it. Let's dance!" Her eyes were glittering strangely.

"Oh honey," I told her, "I can't make it with this music. I can't do nothing to this sound except sit. I've tried. Wait till they play the 'Tennessee Waltz.' "

I was putting her on a bit, so I could remain strung out

on my big idea for Charlotte. It was just as well that I did, too, because unbeknownst to us, Justice and Junior were now out prowling the darkened streets of Mobile in their battered Dodge squad car for a glimpse of my Trans-Am.

Well, they certainly did spot one shiny black model that looked just like mine, parked at the curb side. Justice went and parked right smack in front of it. He jumped out and lifted up the hood and exposed the brand new shiny aluminum engine and ripped out every wire and tube there was, throwing them all on the ground and stomping on them, too, because he knew he didn't want me running out on him another time.

I'm still inside the disco, being badgered for a request by the bandleader who has recognized me.

Request?

I can't hardly hear my own voice, so I go up to the bandstand, at Carrie's insistence, and whisper into the guy's ear to play "Dixie."

So the band starts up real slow about the land of cotton and all, and as soon as all the blacks in the audience hear that one they're heading directly for the exits. So then the leader gives a little nod of his head and a brisk shake sort of, and the band does its changes into a disco beat, and those same blacks are stopped right in their tracks, 16 tracks, as I recall. Then they start in, you should excuse the expression, really boogieing, and Frog has me off on the floor finally, boogieing right along with them.

Well, it wasn't going quite so smoothly for Sheriff Buford outside. That Trans-Am he was busy dismantling in plain view of a streetlight happened to belong to none other than Mr. Ernie Shavers of Mobile, the heavyweight boxing contender; and when he came outside and saw what was happening to his pride and joy automobile, he leaned right over Buford and Junior, nearly shrouding them in his shadow.

So Junior spins around to go back to the sedan for more light, and that was like the very last words of some dying man, because he bumped smack into Shavers' belly button and was sent careening back against his dad.

"You stumblebum idiot," Buford cried out. *"What in the hell do you think you're doing?"*

"That was going to be my very first question to you," says Ernie Shavers.

Justice said, "We've just disabled the *ve*-hickle of a dangerous perpetrator. Now we're on our way to enlist additional forces in the form of lawmen with which to apprehend him."

He started to move but Shavers stepped in front of him again, a big bald mountain of muscle and flesh.

Buford says, "Get your ass out of the way, you big . . ." Then he stopped and looked more closely at Shavers again. "Say, haven't I seen you somewhere before?"

Big Ernie was grinning at him goonishly. "Could be . . ."

"You're . . ."

"Small world, ain't it," went Shavers. "Now about my brand new car over here . . ."

He didn't have to finish his sentence, I do believe, because Justice and Junior got just about that busy right away trying to put all the pieces back together again.

A few hours later, back out in the country just beyond La Mays, I woke up the doc from a deep sleep by Charlotte's side and shoved a cocktail napkin with a drawing scribbled on it right beneath his nose.

I guess it must have looked sort of like the late Ovid Bolus Esquire's slingshot, or maybe one of Parson John Bullen's lizards to him, because before I could say *Christmas* he was screaming, "Help! *Po*-lice . . ."

"Easy Doc," I said, "it's me, Bandit. Just look at this. Don't you think it might work for Charlotte?"

He took my drawing and gave it his most earnest consideration: "*Emmmmmmm. . . .*"

What I had imagined on paper was a sort of netlike cradle which attached to the four corners of the truck with a slit up the middle. I explained as how the net would act like a hemp. We would attach it about five feet high on all sides of the truck and just let Charlotte rest on it with her feet just barely touching the ground and her belly hanging out down through the slit.

Doc got the picture and he said it just might work. But Carrie was irate. "Let me see that infernal machine."

She snatched the drawing out of Doc's hands and then Snowman and even Fred came up, on his hind legs of course, and stared over her shoulder. Snowman said it must be sort of like a giant sling.

"Sling it someplace else," said Frog. "It looks inhuman."

"It ain't supposed to be for a human," I protested. "It's for an elephant and it'll work. Let me ask you something, Frog. What's a big animal with four legs and a trunk?" I demanded.

"*That's irrelevant,*" she said.

"That's a right," I told her. But nobody else was laughing.

Frog said, "If you try to move Charlotte in that bestial contraption, I swear I'm leaving you, Bandit."

She had to know my intentions were honorable and I wasn't going to be threatened. Why did she have to be so damn self-righteous? I was angry and didn't want all our work flushed down the toilet.

"Carrie," I told her, "a man is not a fountain pen. I'm bone tired. You are, too. You know as well as I do the money is what counts. That's why you took the job in the first place, *no*?"

"Why don't you take off your hat more often," she said, "and give your brain some air? You're so stupid Bandit. Do you think I really came with you for the money? I came because I thought you'd changed."

"Why tamper with perfection?" I joked. And I reached out for her. "If you really want me to take off my hat more often, just come with me to a nice quiet motel room and ask."

She wriggled free and slapped me hard in the face. The worst sting of all. Tears sprung to my eyes, but I squinched them back.

Frog said, "You're not cutesie-pieing your way out of this. You're heartless and that's no jo—" She turned and fled to the Trans-Am, where she yanked out her suitcase.

"That's right," I told her. "Walk out on me when things get tough."

"You're forcing me out," Frog said. "I'm not walking

. . ." She didn't look nervous but she seemed to burn with a strange energy. Her face seemed so pale, almost ghostly. The wild curls of her pale hair appeared almost red, like the dazzling lonely crimson of ignited road flares in the night.

"Well, I guess that's a little better," I told her. "Some difference . . . when the gang gets rough, the rough get . . ."

When she spoke again I felt like I was in the Mojave Desert with the Santa Ana blowing. Hot all over . . . and then cold as ice. "Drop dead," went Frog, and she was on her way. She just went over and planted a good-bye kiss on Snowman and Doc, and a kiss and a caress for Charlotte.

Afterwards she said, "I hope you have a very lonely life, Bandit. The odds are good."

Snowman followed her out to the road a short distance. She was going to hitch her way back home, I supposed. I watched them shaking hands on the soft shoulder with a whole lot of sadness. I turned back to Doc and Charlotte again, as Snowman returned.

"What are you all staring at?" I said harshly.

"Nothing," Snowman replied, as he looked hard at my eyes. "Absolutely nothing." I guess even he was a little fed up with me.

I ordered everybody to get the rig set up and ready to go and walked back over to Charlotte, as if to inquire after her well-being. Over the last couple of days she'd become almost human to me, and when I told her that she growled a little, pleasure mixed with displeasure, too.

"No offense," I said. "I just meant you've become so very close to me. So very much part and parcel of my life. So I know you'll understand what I have to do. And what I have to do," I added, "is make money."

I showed my wallet stuffed with unpaid bills. "Look here, big girl," I told her, "liquor shop, landlord, clothes bills. Over two dozen collection agencies sent me Christmas cards, so you gotta know I must turn you over to Big Enos Burdette. You know what I'm doing is right, don't you, Charlotte?"

She shook her head no, emphatically.

The more things change, the more they remain the same, I thought. Frog, I'm so miserable without you already it's almost like your being here, but I managed to say out loud, "Ah, who the hell cares what an elephant thinks anyway?"

After we put the finishing touches on Charlotte's home-made maternity sling, it was just the right height for her feet to touch lightly on the floor. As we struggled to cinch up all the retaining ropes as firmly as possible, her belly rested comfortably in the slit in the middle of the net. I patted her all about and told her rest easy and had the doc stay back with her on call.

Then we took off on the roll again.

XII

Starving the Bears

In the Royal Executive Suite at the Villa Capri motel in Austin, the mark-inside was coming up on the Rube and that's a rumble nobody can tumble. What I mean is, Big and Little Enos were at it again with their damn scam, all together and one at a time.

This is what we picked up about it later. Little Enos was talking away at John Conn over the phone in a closet, like a true closet case, when Big Enos came in from the bedroom and saw the phone wire leading down the living room toward the closet door. He stood outside on his tiptoes and gave a silent listen.

Although the boy was whispering, he could clearly be heard: "Believe me, John. You can donate both the elephant and the Bandit to the San Diego Zoo after this. It's gonna work perfect . . . and while we're talking, I've been thinking about something in a nice orange and white shag rug for the Lieutenant Governor's office—you know, the Texas Longhorn colors." Like the proverbial bum steer in a rage, Big Enos kicked open the door, yanked the phone out of the closet wall, and went into the bedroom and threw it out the window. Then he went back into the closet, grabbed his son, and hugged him tenderly.

"Damn boy, if you don't bring tears to my eyes." He pinches Little's cheek hard. "You make me proud to be a Burdette . . . born and bred."

Hanging from his arms, bewildered, Little timidly said, "I figured you might be just a little sore with me, Daddy."

"Sore? For what? Hell, boy, I'm *proud*. You're a real Burdette. For a long time I've wondered whether you had the guile, the treacherous heart, the larcenous soul, the love of lying, cheating, and stealin' to be a member of this family. But hell, what could be more rotten to the core than betraying your own daddy as he seeks the highest office in Texas?" He then turned a little solemn and said, "Now boy, tell me what that John Conn is up to or I'll stomp your ass 'till it looks like a wet enchilada!"

Little Enos appreciated as how his daddy might not be fooling with him, but he remained defiant. "Go step on your Stetson, Daddy. Till you can offer me something better than Lieutenant Governor, I'm sticking with Big John."

The old man recoiled just like a clenched fist, or a puff adder about to bite. "Boy, you're starting to push this family disloyalty business a mite far."

Buford, meanwhile, was having his own family problems; what you might describe as an inversion of the usual. In Texas at last, he was steaming along after us, somewhere not too far north from Port Arthur in midday. When he pulled off the road behind a Lone Star billboard, which had been set up in advance as a rendezvous point, there was this fruity looking guy in a pale uniform waiting for him. His hair was all white, with a slight purple rinse, and he was exactly where the Sheriff had ordered a stakeout to form up.

"Sorry," he said. "You'll just have to move on. This place is being used for official police work."

"Didn't you send for me, Buford?"

It was his little brother Beauregard standing there, waving at him gayly; and coming around the other side of the billboard was another officer similarly attired with his hair done up in corn rows. They must have both just stepped out of the white late model police cruiser with Texas markings parked nearby.

"You remember, don't you?" Beauregard demanded.

"Sure enough," said Justice. "Never forget a face, even though it's been a few years. You've changed a little."

"Haven't we all," said the fruitcake. "Oh—and this is P.T., my, er, friend."

"What's that P.T. stand for?" Buford asked.

"Perfect ten," went Beauregard.

P.T. passed his tongue along his lips and smiled in a real friendly big city fashion. You could have tied Buford to the Santa Fe railroad and sent him on down to Tucson. He didn't quite know what to say that wouldn't seem rude, so he allowed as how he thought Beau was going to bring him some help.

"Bu," said brother Beau, "I brought my entire force and I already have them all deployed. Nothing could get through the open country we've left uncovered. I met Belvedere in town and took him and his force over, too, so everything is in readiness."

"Anticipation," P.T. winked, as if explaining everything.

Then Beau said, "What a drag this waiting."

"You said it," said Bu.

A car was approaching from a long way off. You could hear the soft flutterings of its engine and, as it came closer, the voices of a man and a woman harmonizing on "Indian Love Call."

"When they're calling you—oooooooo . . . oo—oooo . . ."

Everybody turned in the direction of Memphis, Tennessee as this large red police van approached, with maple leaves along the flash panels and flying from a flag on the antenna, and an RCMP medallion on the hood. The closer it came, the louder was their singing: "If you refuse me then I'll be blue and waiting all alone . . ."

"Who can't refuse that?" said Buford.

"I hope that isn't our Belvedere. But if it is, he fights better than he sings. Daddy brought all of us youngin' up to be lawmen," Beau pointed out. "Just like Momma did you. Belvedere is a credit to the Justice name."

The third member of the Justice clan, Belvedere, had slicked-back dark hair and a slightly larger-than-life Hitler-type moustache. He held the lady beside him close around the waist. She could have been Jeannette MacDonald, with a lot of negative scratch.

"Shall we, my dear?" went number three brother, indicating the rest of the clan where they stood behind the Lone Star billboard. "I haven't seen my brother Bu in 20 years," he continued. "More, if you count the war. What a great way to have a family reunion, bringing law and order to the world."

I think it was Junior who announced then that if this is what they call getting close to your roots, he'd much prefer turnips. He watched his daddy and Belvedere embrace, and then Belvedere and Beauregard and Beauregard and Buford, and he listened to all their greetings, like hog callers getting on the cozy.

"Such a pleasure to see you, Buford. An honor to be called to assist you in the apprehension of this criminal."

"For making that long journey to help one of your own, Belvedere, much thanks."

"We must certainly have a picture of this to show Daddy," says Beauregard. "He'll be so proud. We'll teach you to drink deep before you leave Texas," he added.

They lined up three in a row before the Lone Star stallion. Beauregard said, "P.T., you make sure that camera is working. Who knows when we three shall get together again."

P.T. snapped away and clicked his shutter, until Buford said, "Soft you awhile. About this criminal."

"Relax, Bu," said Belvedere, "as Beau and I have got it all staked out. All you have to do is lead in the sheep."

"And we'll ram it home to him" says Beau, "as this is the very same canyon where our good Daddy caught those cattle rustlers that he told us about so many times."

Buford posed for one last family portrait and then he said, "Brothers, it will be my pleasure to take this sheep to his shearing, so let's save our reunion and rejoicing until after the fact. While you're laying hand to him with manacles, I'll be a nipping at his heels like an old collie dog."

"We'll really put him on the rack," said Beau and

Frenchy, "and then we'll be on our way. We'll be waiting, little brother."

They headed for their cars and left. Justice moved his own car all the way behind the billboard and just waited there.

"Now could I drink hot blood," says Buford. "I've got him. Got him set up for the biggest baddest trap on earth."

"What trap would that be?" asked Junior.

"Texas," he snorts. "That's what big sniveling trap I've got for him."

"Lord sakes alive," goes the twirp. And he points out east, too. "Daddy, hey Daddy."

Well, our little convoy was really steaming the road down flat. Justice hurried out with a big sign he had stashed behind the back seat of his car: WELCOME TO THE LONE STAR STATE. Then he jumps back in his car, guns his motor, and turns out from behind that fence and comes slamming down the road behind us.

Snowman saw him first. "Bandit, we got you-know-who with us again."

But just as he spoke I heard Buford's voice break in. "Tsk, tsk, tsk. It's me against you, Bandit. Best driver wins, with no hard feelings?"

"Do you have any place special you want to drive?" I asked.

"Take the first dirt road," Justice said, "and I'll show you."

"Big ten-four," I told him and hung up. Then I called Snowman. "Cletus, the honkey-donkey is up to something. You keep on rolling, and I'll take him out for the tour."

I cut off the road into rough country with Justice hanging a hard right and following. We moved through a little open country and then down through a wide canyon with sloping walls on either side. I was riding on the dry bed of an old arroyo, going bumpy-dump along, with Buford's springs just about echoing my own.

Over the CB he taunted me. "How's about this pretty scenery, Bandit? We picked it special for you to meet your end down here among the stumbling tumbleweeds. Take a good look around."

To either side of me on the hills were sheriffs' sedans: 25 whites from Beau and 25 reds from Belvedere, and the reds had RCMP markings, too. They was all just laying in wait for me, like a posse for a hanging, or what have you.

I quick got on the tube with Snowman. "Serious trouble down here. County Mounties and Mounty Mounties wall to wall galore. Maybe a C note's worth. Certainly more than I can handle. May Day. May Day. Now listen and listen good. Make that delivery. Get the goods to their destination. Do you read me?"

"Are you serious, Bandit?"

"Shit you not."

"Hang on," says Snowman. "We're on our way."

"Nix. Nix," I say. "Do you copy me right? Just deliver the goods. I'll catch you all later . . . five years or so later, if I'm lucky."

"We don't much fancy it, Bandit," says my good buddy, "but we're streaking west. Hang out all flags and watch out for fags. Stand on it, Bandit."

What happened next was closer to pocket billiards than mere driving. The trap seemed about set, and then I heard Buford screaming like an Indian, "Charge!"

"Bully it is, and charge," went Belvedere.

Buford said, "Your time has come!"

And then Beau chimed in, "Beaver patrol to the rescue, charge!"

Well, they all started down the incline of that canyon my way, with Buford in hot pursuit. What a sight that must have been, more like Custer's last stand than a chase. A procession of fire ants and great white slugs after my ass.

Inside my Trans-Am, I put one hand to the dashboard and my foot on the blow-pedal. Took a deep snuffle of air-cooled air and said, "Little black beauty, don't you fail your old buddy now."

Off I went with police cars gathering in bunches on either flank of me. Good thing I still had my CB on the right channel, because when I heard Belvedere tell some of his boys to "plug that little hole in front," I pushed all the harder and squeezed on through. But they stayed on my tail in a pack.

"Hey Bandit," Justice says, "seems like you can run, but can you hide?"

I shouted back, "You may get me, Sheriff, but I do surely hope you've got this fleet of yours covered with full comprehensive because, believe me, we're gonna bend some metal before this one's over."

Looking straight ahead then, I saw this semi coming right at me and it was Snowman alright. "You damn fool," I yelled. "Didn' I tell you to haul ass?"

"Hey pardner. When we set out to do a job together, we do a job, and we do it together."

"Well maybe they'll send us to the same penitentiary." He was heading straight at that convoy of police cars, standing on all his horns as he went.

Snowman said, "It really ain't over yet, pardner. How many trucks do you see?"

I sure as hell was baffled and buggered. "One. When there's one Cletus, I only see one, unlest I been drinking."

"Look again, good buddy. Okay boys," Showman added, "do it to it!"

From behind Snowman's rig and fanning out across the turf in one straight line, like the cavalry at Fort Apache, came an incredible, colossal, endless fleet of semis, all barreling their way toward that red and white convoy. As the two massive formations headed straight for a cataclysmic collision that would have made the sinking of the Titanic into a tempest in a tosspot, Snowman bellowed forth, "Welcome to the world's largest game of chicken, boys."

But, seconds before such a collision could occur, all 100 cars executed a massive 180-degree turn and hauled ass away. I slipped on through, but Snowman and his buddies went chasing after the cops.

He was chortling away like an unstuck drain. "Absent me from felicity awhile, Bandit. It worked. We got them honkies on the run."

I saw Snowman and his gang were really gaining ground on the smaller sedan pack. I threw a 180-degree myself, and headed for the action. "Save some of it for me, Snowman."

The rest was wham-bam-and-thank-you-Mister-Sheriff: a classic can-can battle, John Wayne versus the Indians. We went about slamming from car to car and pretty soon they were slamming against each other and even turning over without our having to put any metal to them.

The carnage of that chase was all to the cars; nobody much got hurt. According to Snowman, who checked, the doc and Charlotte were able to hang on throughout and didn't even get a scratch. But it left me to thinking what kind of a life is this and what kind of a sport: smashing headfirst into other vehicles? Better I should stay in bed than cause so much mayhem, even though it was sorta fun. After all, a man is more than the sum of all his parts, right? I had compassion. No doubt about it, and I really didn't want anybody getting hurt.

We'd taken the jousting day for sure and most of the realm just fled in panic. Even Snowman began to have his qualms about those 20 wrecked cars that were lying all about because it was such a waste of honest human labor and materials. So, when I said I'd had about all the fun I could have for one day, he told me, "I'll lead out of here Bandit."

He broke away from the milling vehicles and out across the open countryside with me following him. Well, Justice saw us split, but how to put a handle to it? He believed there was no way out of that canyon and he led his two brothers in pursuit of us.

Ahead was the ravine, a seemingly impenetrable barrier. We pressed on, nevertheless, and then I saw a fleet of ten long semis lying in the ravine so as to form up a bridge, and I hurtled across their backs right behind Cletus.

When my tires hit the dirt again, Snowman was yammering on the tube, "That was perfect, drivers. Hope we can do the same for you someday."

"A real truckin' treat, Snowman," came a girl's voice back at us. "All good numbers to you and Bandit. Like wow."

The Justice boys were speeding behind us toward that same truck bridge, but when the last three semis pulled out of line, they leaped and tumbled out of sight, leaving us all with only a sound of crunching metal.

XIII

Love Without Fear

Somewhere west of Dallas, Charlotte's water broke and Snowman told me Doc said she was about to have her baby. Doc complained he was getting pretty nervous now that Charlotte's time was drawing nigh.

"We better stop and take us a peek as soon as we can," I said.

We'd passed Irving and The Seven Flags Over Texas, and beyond was a tract of semi-detached bungalows, wedged in next to the back end of one of those Lion Country safari-type operations. As we drove past we could hear the muffled roaring of the great beasts, and I thought, under the circumstances, this must be the place.

With Snowman following, I pulled in through the main gate, got out, and latched the postern behind us. I didn't want battered old Buford following us in here, claiming he'd been following a star or something. For this manger scene we'd have nothing but the call of the wild.

Fact is, all that remained of poor Buford's sedan was the frame and its engine, which was spewing smoke like bees from a hive. That car had been pulverized and crushed up no more than six feet long, so Buford had to lean way back even to see the road. Next to him, Junior, with his hair blowing in the wind like a flag of defeat, was making siren noises louder and louder, just as his daddy had ordered him to do.

Around Irving they came to a vast line of traffic waiting to park for a Texas Rangers' doubleheader, and Buford—totally without brakes—rear-ended the last vehicle on the line, sending Junior sailing up toward heaven. There was a patrolman standing nearby and he came running to the scene of the "perpetration."

"How do," says Bu, with a sickly smile like he's about to throw up, "offosir, don't I know you? My name's . . ."

"I still don't care if your name's Broderick Crawford."

Justice told his son, "Does any of this sound familiar to you, Junior?"

"Don't you know," says Officer Wise, "you can't drive a piece of shit like that on our highway?"

"I'll thank you not to use that kind of language in my presence," Buford says, "and in the presence of my youngin'."

"Look, mister, I'm asking you one simple . . ."

"Hold it," says Buford.

"Goddamn."

"I said hold it," Buford said. "Don't you ever raise your voice to me. Do you know who you're talking to? I happen to be Buford T. Justice, a distinguished officer of over 30 years seniority . . . one of the most highly respected law enforcement agents in the United States of America."

Quite crestfallen, the officer started to apologize. "Sir, I'm sorry . . . I . . . well, I . . . I had no idea. . . . It never occurred to me. Well, please, sir. You proceed immediately. Oh, sir, I . . . I hope you'll accept my apologies for my profanity."

"Apologies accepted," says Buford. "*Now fuck off*."

For the birthing of Charlotte's youngin', meanwhile, all the animals in Safari Kingdom assembled. It was like that Christmas card painting of the Peaceable Kingdom: giraffes laying down with lionesses, and hippos with gazelles. Everybody perfectly well-behaved, too; just keeping to themselves. This was going to be the first elephant ever born in the Kingdom. Peering out from the bushes surrounding the clearing where Charlotte lay on her side were camels, bears, zebras, tigers, and giraffes.

We all helped out, of course. I spread a huge ground sheet from my trunk across her middle and Snowman wiped Charlotte's brow. Doc kept checking her progress nervously, and Fred ushered stray animals into place.

I must have smoked three straight cigars out of nervousness. That scene would have melted Disney's heart, but it was giving me heartburn and excess acid.

I kept asking the doc, "How much longer?"

He was pretty darn nonchalant about his reply. "Well, since an elephant's gestation period is about twice as long as a woman's, I'd have to say it may take twice as long as it would for a woman. Of course, I am not a veterinarian."

"Well, how long would it take *for a woman*?" I asked.

"I don't know. I'm not an obstetrician, either. You know," he went on, "it's like asking me how long will a man lie in the ground before he rots."

"Don't be morbid," I said. "How long?"

"Depends on their trade. A tanner will take a long, long time because his skin is so tanned with his trade . . . whereas a C.I.A. agent, for example, may be rotten through and through right from the beginning."

"Are you some kind of communist?" I demanded.

"Bull," said the Doc. "I'm a medical man. I'm for life, not death. Now let me see to Charlotte."

He ducked his head under the sheet again, and I continued to pace. Suddenly I heard a squeal of brakes and flinched. I learned later it was Buford coming to a quick stop in front of our Trans-Am, but just then it set me all into a tizzy.

"You sure are nervous," Snowman said.

"Who wouldn't be?" I shrugged. "This is my very first elephant."

Right at that moment Buford and Junior were thrashing through the jungle brush beating a path to Charlotte's lying-in.

I thought to myself, pull her through this, Doc, and I'll be nice to Frog. I won't fool around anymore. I'll look her up and be good to her. Just pull her through, Doc, and give me a healthy elephant and child and you'll see what a damn mensch

I'll be. I'll be good to Frog and good to Charlotte and good to everybody under the sun I'll even consider obeying traffic laws.

Familiarity breeds love. I got to feeling close to Charlotte in a way, good about her. I wanted her to make it soon, without any further discomfort, healthy and happy.

I lit another cigar and damn near drew on the lit match and threw away the stogie.

Suddenly I heard Doc's voice, "It's a boy!"

He was holding a pink new baby elephant up to the beams of the truck headlights and gently slapping its bottom to get it to cry.

There was nothing for all of us to do except cheer. Even the assembled animals were making appropriate noises. A cute little baby boy elephant: new life in the primeval forest implanted there by Leisure Industries, a division of Gulf & Western.

It was a miracle that lived and breathed, dangled its trunk, and made little snuggly sounds. I was impressed by the Creation as I had never been by the destruction. Amazing Grace, as we darn near always used to say.

Abruptly, I saw Justice and Junior at the edge of the forest, and the Sheriff had drawn his gun: "This whole goddamn jungle is under arrest."

Woe is me, I thought, raising my hands high when he jammed his gun into my ribs. But when she saw me being threatened, Charlotte, even though she was nursing, bellowed, and reared, and wrapped her trunk around Justice's leg, and flung him sky high and down into the nearest pond.

At first Justice sunk, but then he reemerged and splashed about and started sinking in again, so Junior came a-running from the bushes and leaped into the pond to save his daddy.

"Daddy," he cried, "Daddy!"—all agaggle like a big blond goose.

Time was once again wasting. Charlotte, having performed her good deed, was settling down against the sod to nurse. I started hustling everybody into action. "Let's load Charlotte up and get her to that convention."

"Load her up?" The doc was agitated. "She can't stand. What about her baby?"

"We'll leave him right here. It's sure a right perfect spot for him to grow up," I explained. "Come on."

I went over to pat Charlotte's spindly shanked little boy as he struggled to hold himself up.

The doc said, "Mr. Bandit, I'm going to have to put my foot down. This baby is too young to be separated from his mother."

"Woodman spare that tree," I scoffed.

"Now listen good, Bandit," Snowman said. "I went along with a lot of hard-hearted moves during this gig, but I ain't gonna be no part of separating a mother and her newborn suckling babe."

"You are absolutely right," I said. "Absolutely. We can't separate them, so let's throw them both into the truck together, as it were. . . ."

"You don't seem to understand," the doc said. "My professional reputation is at stake. This is also a very delicate time for both mother and child. There could be complexes later on. We shouldn't try to move them right away."

I opined as how Charlotte looked strong as an ox.

"She *is* strong as an ox," said the doc. "Now we have to wait a little while until she's as strong as an elephant."

So we argued back and forth. I argued that if we waited any longer, we'd be too late to make the convention. Snowman argued that moving mother and son right now was indecent, and the doc said it was risky, too.

"If you're finished, *reverend*," I told Cletus, "I got a job to do."

I pushed my way past Snowman toward where Charlotte lay. But just as I came up close, I saw a fist and felt it hit my jaw like a ton of bricks. Snowman had knocked me flat out. He told the doc, "It's one of the many services I perform for my esteemed buddy. Once in a while I have to knock some sense back into him."

Be that as it may, lying there flat out like an old carpet didn't do very much for my self-esteem. Then I heard a sound I can only describe as a cross between a belch and a sob, and I felt an enormous drop of water land on my brow with a salty splash. I glanced up and there was Charlotte, weeping for my plight.

She was crying real hard, and they weren't crocodile tears that were landing in a downpour all over me. I never could stand to see a woman cry, and I told her so: "Don't. Now please don't."

But she wouldn't stop, and then her little baby also joined in. I really couldn't take it any more. They were getting to me. You know what they say about a mother's kisses. Well, it's twice as much with tears.

"All right, all right," I said. "Man can only stand so much. Screw Big Enos," I said. "Are we gonna sell what's left of our souls just so he can get that fat ass into the Statehouse? Charlotte," I said, "stays with us."

Those elephants stopped their weeping pronto.

The doc asked, "You mean it, Bandit?"

"I've seen the light," I pointed out. "There's more to life than money and power. . . . There's . . . there's . . ." If they'd given me another minute, I'd have thought of something. But we had other things to do. I left the doc to guard our mother and child and went off with Snowman to find a U-Haul.

Justice and Junior were still thrashing about in that mudpond when we drove by them, but they were in no real danger. Only trouble was this lion; every time they tried to climb out, he pawed at the rim of the pond and growled something fierce.

I guess the moral of this story should be love conquers all, or the elephant never forgets. But there's a lot more to it than that. Love is mammoth; never deny the love of a female be she beast or woman, or you'll live to regret it. Not to mention, make hay while the sun shines or the elephants will get all of it.

A few days later I was driving up near Texarkana in the Trans-Am pulling two U-Haul trailers, one for Charlotte and one for her kiddo, Nathan. Snowman, Fred, and Doc, were taking up our rear in the semi.

Out at the Four Corners where the road goes Tulsa one way and Dallas the other, a young woman was sitting on a bench with a suitcase, waiting for the bus. I blew my horn because it was Frog.

When she looked up and saw us all—no doubt about it—there was love in her eyes. Happy love, mingling with desire, too. She came at us on the dead run.

Well, I got out of the Trans-Am and we embraced in the middle of that street, but as I explained to her afterwards, "Damn . . . I had this saintly expression I wanted you to see . . . but now my thoughts ain't so pure."

"Bueno," Frog said. "Good."

We climbed into the Trans-Am together and drove off with Charlotte and Nathan trumpeting in unison behind us.

A happy caravan that was, I tell you, but just as we started off toward Tulsa, this Tulsa-bound bus caught up alongside us. Sitting in the driver's seat wearing a crushed hat was Sheriff Buford T. Justice himself, screaming, "I'll get you yet, you sommamamabitch!"

I pulled away and left him in the dust. But I won't say his greeting didn't stick with me. Although Buford was always that way, I suppose, he sure had his reasons for having it in for me, not to mention Big and Little Enos Burdette. As they say, a good man can make enemies just for breathing, and a man like me who isn't always so good sometimes doesn't even have to take a breath.

In my scam, sometimes happiness is just a sheriff put out of work. Anyway, my troubles with Buford began a long, long time ago when I was still sowing my wild oats, and he made it his business to put a fig leaf over every one of my halcyon days. That was the so-called era of good feeling between me and most Smokies. The world shone like a big red apple, and the only way station between me and any woman I ever met was the Moon itself. It was a time, as the old song says, "when the mountain laurel blushed to see the dogwood so out front. . . ."

When I got back from that cross country elephant stampede, there was a letter waiting for me at my motel. It was from this woman I'd been seeing sometimes. B.F., which means Before Frog.

Dear Pandit Bandit,
Long time no hear from me, huh?
There's good news and there's bad news.

The good news is I'm getting married again.
The bad news is I won't be able to see you anymore.
Don't know if that's as bad for you as it is for me.
Every trucker between here and Denver has been telling me about that piece of fluff you been seen burning up the blacktop with.
Frog, you say. Frog my fanny. I hope you're very happy with her is all I can say.
Bandit, my new man is a coal-mining man.
Loomis is his name and he's big and strong.
You come sniffing around my house any more, yore likely to get pole-axed.
Not to say I won't think of you often with love and kindness.
Ginger

To tell you the truth, my mind was so fogged up by then I couldn't quite remember if Ginny was the person I thought she was, and when, if ever, I met Frog. The truth was, it seemed to me she really was Forever. But putting two plus two together as best I can, this is what I seem to recall.

It was the best of times; it was the worst of times. The Vietnam war was a thing of the past and we were all still living with after-effects, like shell-shock victims.

So one day I was working a rodeo down by Wichita Falls when this big white customized Caddy sporting license plates that read MR. BIG drives up to the place where I had slung my hammock, and out step Big and Little Enos Burdette again. They're dressed as identical rhinestone cowboys, garish as all hell and they're looking for me.

Well, I must have thought they were trying to get even for my failure to deliver the elephant, but that hadn't even happened yet. Truth was, Frog wasn't in my life yet either; I was just plain confused and in a tizzy. I was working rodeos like this for $25 a day, a living legend, and poor as hell, too, with nothing much more to call my own than old Tiger, my first cherry-colored Trans-Am with the cherry-wood fittings, plus the clothes on my back, some faded denims, and silver-toed shitkicker boots.

When I wanted to take a nap between performances, I

slung myself out on that hammock from down Mexicali way and placed a cowboy hat over my face. Hard times in the country, as they say in the old song. Days of Sneaky Pete and posies. I was even into going around just then with a Oklahoma state trooper who happened to be named Pachasandra, only I called her Sandy for short. Pretty little thing, but we rarely saw much of each other, as she was on nightside when I was day, and vice versa.

So there I was, lying out in my hammock in this pecan orchard, dreaming sweet dreams of night turning to day, or vice versa, with maybe $5.75 cash to my name, when I hear these two unmistakably Texican voices: "See there boy? Old legends never die—they just lose weight." He leaned across my prone body. "Next time you get a chance, boy, eat something."

I was a little miffed for having my nap interrupted, but I didn't move an eyelash.

"Daddy," says the other voice, "now don't you dare disturb the Bandit."

"Disturb?" bellowed the first of them. "He ain't hardly quivering. This here's an attraction at the meet. They gonna set up a booth here and sell tickets to look at a living legend. If you notice, son, a living legend and an outta-work bum look just about the same." He jostled hard at my hammock. "BANDIT, ME AND MY SON IS HERE," he hollered. "BIG ENOS TALKING TO YOU, BANDIT, FROM BURDETTE, TEXAS."

Slowly, I raised my Stetson and revealed my huge boyish grin and looked them over: a couple of rubes dressed up as Christmas trees for sure. Under my gaze, father and son turned a little fidgety. Even the old man's shadow looked overweight; it seemed to have trouble climbing up my hammock when he backed away a bit.

I said, "Love those suits, fellas. Must be mighty hard to find a 58 extra fat . . . not to mention the 12 dwarf."

"As I would remind you," said the fat man then, "I'm Big Enos Burdette and this is my son, Little Enos."

"Never use the stuff," I said.

"DO YOU KNOW WHO YORE TALKIN' TO?"

"I'll bet."

I closed my eyes again. Little Enos must have thought he was being insulted, because he started toward me, and then got scared and turned to his daddy, Big Enos, for an explanation. He seemed to be in a terrible confusion. Something about hell boiling over, or words to that effect.

He says to me, "Mr. Bandit, I kin spit a blister onto a washpot ontil the flies blow hit." Whatever that was supposed to mean.

Big Enos told me, "You mighty lippy for a man what used to be."

"That's 'cause," I said, "I'm talking to a man what never was . . . and never will be," I added for Little Enos' benefit.

He wasn't hearing none of it. "Bandit, my daddy will climb in that hammock after you."

"Your mamma already did," I pointed out.

"Hush up now," said Big Enos. "I cum here not to hassle you, but to make a deal. What do you think he gets, boy, if he's lucky enough to win this goddamn trucker's rodeo?"

"If?" I asked.

Little Enos thought maybe five thou, which was frankly a bit high, I thought.

Big Enos said, "Chickenshit money." He coughed like he was just about to lay an egg himself.

I hid my face behind my hat and said, "Could you kindly turn your head next time?"

"BULLSHEEEIT," said the big man, so I got up and started unhooking my hammock. I was going to lay myself down someplace else.

Big Enos asked, "What's round like a pecan with fur all over it?"

"Don't you talk dirty to me," I said.

"Stick with me and you can have all you'll ever want," he said.

"Lookit," I told him, "I ain't in this truck rodeo for the money. It's the challenge that gets to me. You know what I mean, ecstasy of victory, agony of defeat."

Big Enos wasn't buying. "You like money, Bandit, and I know you do. You're gonna have an elephant to feed some day, and I really can't believe there's two thousand people out here in the stands ready to watch a bunch of guys backing up their trucks."

"America's bored," I said. "Nothing else to do." I turned away. "Now what's on your mind?"

"You," Big Enos said. "Just you. You're to forget this silly rodeo and take on a real challenge."

"You want me to go Air Force or something?" I asked, I turned again and walked away, but they followed me.

They just wouldn't take no for an answer. They had this scam and they wanted it done. Drive to Texarkana and come back with a load of Coors beer in less than 28 hours.

Sort of a brew-ha-ha.

No problems ordinarily, except for some scruples I might have had, as I tried to explain.

"Twenty-eight hours to Texarkana and back is no problem," I said, "but running Coors beer east of Texas is what do bother me. Sort of makes me into a bootlegger."

"And what are you now?" Big Enos asked.

"A bootlegger some of the time, and sometimes I'm also a living legend of speed and agility. It wouldn't pay to get my reputation so besmirched if I landed in the slammer."

Little Enos told me he thought I was just plain scared.

"Wonderful psychology," I told him. "Why don't you also say something about my mother?"

"Your mother."

"Quiet boy," Big Enos says. Again he coughed, as if I'd wrecked him, or somebody had. "Lookit now, Mr. Bandit," he went on, "you make this little run for me, and I'll . . . now let me see . . . I'll . . . a new rig costs about 80 thou. Close to three grand an hour, if you can make it in 28 hours. Now would that be challenge enough for you?"

Demur no longer, Bandit, I told myself, especially when I saw Little E. looking so startled, sputtering, "Pop. Pop."

"Never mind boy," the fat man said. "Pop goes the weasel."

But even I was, how you say it, incrudulent, or whatever.

"Are you crazy?" I asked. "Why do you want all this barley pop so bad?"

"He's just thirsty," said Junior. I smiled at Little Enos and tickled him under the chin.

Then Big Enos allowed as how he would explain all. "It was a dark stormy night, the captain said to the crew . . ."

"Now cut it out," I said, "or I'm splitting."

"Easy Bandit," he said, "and I'll explain all. It's really very simple. Got a boy running in the Peach Tree classic tomorrow and when he wins, I wanna celebrate in style."

I asked how much style.

"Reckon 400 cases worth will do," he told me. "Well?"

I wanted cash on the barrelhead and I said it.

He took it as an insult. "The word of Big Enos is good as gold. Ask anybody."

"What about the corpse of Big Enos?" I demanded.

"Give him, boy," the fat man said.

Little Enos took out a wad of bills the size of a thermometer and they was all hundreds. He started dealing into my palm.

I said, "I'll also need a car to run blocker and some money for the beer."

"Deal, boy, deal," Big Enos said. "This is one big deal."

XIV

In the Boonies

Cletus lived way back in the boonies, in rattlesnake country, in an area of lush green meadows and endless piney woods. Up around Chickamauga there are deep glens and a lot of creeks and lakes. Far back in those secluded vastnesses, among lowing cattle and wild boars, Cletus stashed his large and growing family in a big rambling clapboard structure of weathered white pine.

I'd come to grab him for company on the road, and when I parked down by the cow barn, among all the ruined car hulks, and ran outside toward the porch, Cletus' woman, Waynette, was waiting for me at the front door, bedecked in 40 pounds of curlers and an old pongee wrapper.

If she was surprised to see me, she certainly wasn't all that happy about it. The door flew open. Waynette was sweeping out the trash.

"Beautiful!" I greeted her, smiling, with my arms wide open.

Waynette slammed the door in my face.

"I meant *gorgeous*," I added, and this time I grabbed the door before she could latch it shut and pushed it open wide.

"You *cain't* have him," Waynette said, backing her

way into the living room as if she was protecting Cletus from the state police.

What a menagerie that was, I tell you: toys, diapers, cribs, live children and their pets underfoot everywhere. Cletus had been in Nam where, like so many, he got a touch of cancer from Agent Orange defoliant (remember that?)—which only goes to prove you can't keep a good man down, in the words of the old song, because Waynette wasn't through with what he could give her even now. Waynette seemed to be planning to have even more younguns.

"You cain't have him," she repeated. "You really can't." She blocked my way to the bedroom where Cletus lay still fast asleep.

I glanced around the disorder. It was slightly overwhelming. "Looks like *you* can. . . . What are you two doing—starting a new race?"

"Leave us alone," Waynette said. "You got Cletus in jail once. Ain't that enough?"

"Waynette," I pointed out, "it wasn't exactly my fault."

"Nothing ever is," she said.

"I was in love."

"With the wife of the Mayor of Nashville, Tennessee as I recall," she said.

"Hush up," I said. "There are children around."

"I'll say all I please," went she. "You were in love. So what did you do? Did you stop fooling around? Did you quit work? Nothing of the sort." She shook her curlers at me. "I'll tell you what you did. You had Cletus leave home and get in trouble to help you out. I've always said, I've never met a man who would interrupt his damn career because of a love affair, or a woman who wouldn't . . . *do just that*. That poor mayoress," she added.

"Be that as it may," I told her, "where is Cletus?"

"None of yire damn business," Waynette said.

Just then a scrawny little kid ran through the room, followed by an even scrawnier mutt nipping at his heels. "Hi there, Uncle Bandit."

Waynette turned livid. "He ain't your damn uncle. He's no kin at all to us and get that mutt outta here. He just peed all over my wet sheets." Then she turned on me. "Bandit, you cad, you look at me."

"I can't Waynette." I pointed at her curlers. "I always think you're busy listening to a radio station in Savannah."

"You let Cletus alone," she told me. "This is my home! Besides, he ain't a well man."

"Just because they removed one lump," I told Waynette, "don't mean the whole game's over, as you well know Waynette."

"This is my home," she insisted. "My abode!"

My Lord, was I fresh with her. "I see it darlin'. And you've done some wonderful things with plastic."

She was now between a rock and a hard place and I leaned toward her in a conspiratorial way. "You know, darlin', you could cut down on a kid-a-year if you took some of that plastic and wrapped it around Cletus—you know where. . . ."

Without any further ado, or even a toodle-oo, I entered the Snowman's bedroom. The bump beneath the loaf of quilts, covers, and comforters was no ordinary sick person. He breathed slowly and easily and snored like a woman after love-making. I shook him gently somewhere near the shoulders. "Cletus?"

"No."

"You know I never would again lead you the wrong way."

"Hey, no," he said with muffled rage, not wishing to be disturbed.

"Cause we learned our lesson the last time," I pointed out. "Right?"

"Righto," he said. "No!"

"But," I interrupted, "I just got us a hot run for really big bucks. About 8-0 thousand of them."

"There are things a man must do," Cletus said, leaping from bed to pull on his trousers, "for the sake, if nothing else, of his posterior."

"Posterity," I corrected him.

"Whatta we have to do," he asked, "kidnap the Pope?"

"How did you know?"

I helped Cletus to dress himself. He was still pretty

much out of it. "Look, all we gotta do," I pointed out, "is make a run to Texarkana and pick up 400 cases of Coors . . . in 28 hours," I added under my breath.

"That's illegal," Cletus pointed out. "Running Coors is bootlegging."

"The Old Bandit and Snowman team can do it and you know it."

"But I got a run to make to Valdosta," he said. "Good run. Runt pigs."

"Also boring," I pointed out.

Cletus asked, "Why the hell we wantta run Coors from Texas?"

"It's the good old American way of life," said I. "Lotta fun and a lotta glory." I leaned far over him as I helped him lace up his boots. "And enough money for a new rig. We're back in business, boy!"

Outside, the kids were screaming like a massacre was taking place.

Cletus hollered, "Waynette!"

In the dining room, Waynette protested loudly. "This ain't fair. You're letting this Bandit talk you into something."

"I'll be back before you know it, pumpkin, I swear to God," said Cletus. "And then," he added with a giggle, "I'll make you glad you're a woman."

"Well I just might not be here."

We moved out toward the porch. "Honey, don't be that way," Cletus said. "You know I'd do anything for you."

"*Anything*?" That scrawny little tyke Alfie had just knocked a flower pot off the window sill. Fred, the dog, was nosing all the bulbs as though they were milkbones. Waynette scooted over and picked up Alfie with one hand and Fred with the other. "*Anything Cletus*?" she insisted.

"Anything, little darlin', pumpkin, baby love."

"Don't you sweet talk me, you big lug," said Waynette. "Just take Fred off with you and give Alfie a . . . a licking," she added.

So sure enough, Cletus went over to his son in Waynette's arms and tongued the boy's face all over with soppy wet kisses. Then he kissed all the other children, one at a time, and Waynette and Fred, too. As we left the house with Fred, he told me, "Believe me, bub, Fred'll be no problem."

As if he had to convince *me*. I'm not much of a dog lover, but I'm certainly no dog hater. I used to feel the same way about children: the less the more.

I told Cletus, "A major asset, that Fred, no doubt about it . . . I can tell."

We put him in the front seat of the truck and stood around figuring our signals. Driving 900 miles each way in 28 hours would require some coordination. As usual, Snowman would drive his rig and I'd run blocker in my little cherry-colored beauty. But Cletus had some alterations to suggest in the way we signaled each other over CB. I was to be Bandit I, and he would be Bandit II. Near as I could figure it out, if he said to go to channel three he really meant channel six, and 21 meant 19, and channel two meant one. Pretty confusing stuff. Maybe the Pittsburgh Steelers could fool with that sort of thing, but not old Bandit.

"Listen," I said. "Let's just stay on the odd channels and switch upward every time. We can start in the basement. Now let's haul ass."

I jumped in the Trans-Am and revved up, laying down a strip of rubber Cletus could have bounced along in his rig.

XV

Boone Hagandas

Wall to wall and treetop tall, we rode down through Alabama to Mississippi and down into the Delta. Cotton and soy bean country, mostly; rich dark soil, and where there were once slaves doing stoop labor, now there are big air-conditioned machines. A few are doing well hauling ass on these machines, but most are just as dirt poor and sore as ever. Pellagra country: the land of sickle cell neglect.

My folks once farmed down here just before the first big war, having bought up a whole bunch of land from a certain Colonel Sartoris. He went bust and got killed in a duel and the mortgage was held by a local family name of Snopes. Pa had it out with Flem, the top man. Pa wanted to stay on, but to do so he would have to share crop and Flem would get the lion's share, just the way he treated his slaves, Pa said. The property was taken out from under us and rented to a yellow-eyed mulatto, half-Indian, named Boone Hagandas and his spindly looking daughter, Eudora, who might still be there for all I know.

Driving along ahead of Snowman, with Fred riding shotgun behind me, I became melancholy thinking of those old times, and how far I had come up from the dirt, and how far I still had to go. Spotted horses wouldn't be able to catch me once I got really started. It would be like running from a burning barn.

The lugubrious mood hung over me, nevertheless. I had to break its spell. I told Snowman, "Gonna run a couple of miles ahead of you. Keep both feet on the floor. We'll be moving 90 and over."

"Bandit?" Cletus' voice sounded honestly troubled, perplexed, bothered in the extreme.

"*Yeah?*"

"Why are we doing all this?" he asked plaintively.

"Why not?"

"They said it couldn't be done, Bandit."

"Then that's the reason. Call it, if you like," I added, "another small step up for humankind." Because, you see, a certain jauntiness helped me deal with my melancholy and I chose to accept the End of Humankind.

As I sped along suspended inside my safety harness, sipping coffee from a Thermos direct without the intervention of a cup, I listened to a driving Cajun Doug Kershaw fiddle tune on the AM band, which cheered me considerably. All the Smokies we passed by day seemed to be going the other way with other things on their mind. So we had a straight shot and let her roll. Bear traps are harder to see at night but we rolled on anyway, deep inside Arkansas.

We drove on all night long through Arkansas. Those Smokies all had their gumball machines working, but none of them could catch us, much less stop us. Once I got chased below Fort Smith by a gumball and ducked behind a building lot as he went past, crashing right into the state of Oklahoma.

So then we hit the diagonal and headed southwest. Night was fading slowly into day when we both blasted across the state line, 900 miles later, and saw that big welcome sign:

TEXARKANA, TEXAS WELCOMES YOU

Certainly nothing arcane about that, or about the place where the beer was stashed, which was in a large dark warehouse right smack in the center of the outskirts of town. The place was locked up and dark when we arrived. The loading dock was empty. We'd be hours here just waiting.

Cletus said we were at least an hour ahead of schedule.

"Let's keep it that way," I said, grabbing for a crowbar.

Inside the warehouse it was black as pitch. When I crossed over to the wall to grope for a light switch and hit it up flat-handed, the entire room was suddenly bathed in fluorescent. Case upon case of Coors met my eyes, like a wall of aluminum medallions. I called it Liquid Gold, but Cletus said it was more like Redneck Heaven.

The reason why Rednecks like Coors so much over Lone Star, for example, or Schmitz, or Rolling Rock, is you don't get too heavy a head. It's sort of light and bubbly and don't look like you've been swallowing detergent suds. Harder to trace when you're coming home late at night and decide to red eye the darkness with your initials in the dirt before turning in. Well maybe, but I always thought it was so much less filling myself, and we now have to fill a whole trailer with 400 cases of it, by hand if necessary.

There was a new fork-lift standing by and Cletus wanted to know if I knew how to make it go.

"Can a pig whistle?" I asked. "Is the Pope Jewish?"

But I climbed aboard the seat and turned the ignition key—baroom, baroom. Grinning I threw the thing into gear. Like some klatoo monster, the forks lifted and it went forward like R2D2 instead of backwards as I'd been hoping it would.

Damn thing was uncontrollable. It went smash in every direction except the one I thought I was aiming it at, and the cases of brews were cascading down as in an avalanche, flying out everywhere, and tossing me out of my seat right on my ass.

"Hold on hoss," said Cletus, racing up behind it to turn off the ignition key so it just sat there, after a big backfire, its fork settling down slowly toward the cement floor.

I was on the ground, surrounded by beer cans. Cletus said, "So much for whistling pigs and Jewish popes."

We were a little ahead of the game so we started loading up Bandit II by hand. That took nearly a whole hour, I guess, and toward the end Cletus had gotten the hang of the fork-lift and we were able to make pretty good time. I suggested we get the hell out of there right away.

"Shouldn't we pay them for the damages?" Cletus asked.

"Righto," I said. I took my felt tip and scribbled all across the whitewashed wall: "Bill to Big Enos Burdette, Burdette, Texas."

Didn't take us no time to get back out of Texarkana loaded. Hell, that's one town I've been loaded in more times than I care to count.

So now we were rolling along through the hog country backlands, 20 minutes ahead of our own schedule, and feeling good and easy with only 900 or so miles to go. It was still a long haul we had, but we were clear and rolling.

Not too far from the turn off for Maud, on the by-pass headed south, there's a village called Onomatopoeia. It's a funny little place where everybody sounds just like what he or she does: the plumber is called Mr. Plug, and the grocer lady is Mrs. Ringading, and there's a dairy owned by the Lowing Bros., and a sow bristle factory which the Honk brothers presently run. Don't ask me why. Goes back a long ways to when they was immigrants. Must have been some sort of religious belief: to sound just like what you do in life. Things could be worse, I should think.

Well, right between Maud and Momfred, as I was trying to by-pass that silly old hamlet, we were going down a certain back country road not too far from the Old Age Home, and my thoughts were turning morbidly to death and dissolution, when there in the middle of the road in a beautiful fussy white wedding gown was just about the prettiest girl I ever saw in my whole life. Not beautiful, mind you, but pretty and wholesome like a bread ad.

Off to one side behind her was a Camaro with a late model set of rims, a "Just Married" sign on the back, and strings of tin cans, shoes, and streamers hanging down off it. The Camaro's hood was up, but my motor was running. I eased up on the accelerator to move around the girl, but she moved with me, a lady in distress, and sort of agile, too.

Here I was then, in the middle of my life and on the road, just as they say, when I was smitten by how beautiful she was, not just pretty, but truly beautiful and bop and slick and a little weird, too, all flounced out like that in white. I thought of my old Eyti road-running friend, Dante Caligari, of East

St. Louis, Missouri. What would he have made of this? The skirt was practically trying to have me run her over from the way she was blocking my path. I squeezed the stop box and she rushed to open my side door.

Look who's coming through the door, as the old song says: "Hello Love. Hello Love."

"Sorry," I told her, as a joke, if nothing else, "but I don't want to get married."

"Terrific," she glared. "That makes two of us." She slammed the door and ran back to her own car, pulled a hat box out of the back seat, ran back, threw her hatbox in the back storage space, came inside, sat down, and turned and said, "Wherever you're going will be fine with me. Drive."

I think my jaw was stuck at permanently ajar. I had to use my other hand to close my mouth.

She said, "Does this move?"

"You bet your ass, girl," said I, zooming off.

I think she got more than she bargained for initially. When I took turns at 85 mph she looked mighty scared. But beautiful and scared, if you know what I mean. After a few minutes of silence I decided to get her story. "Let me guess," I said, "you want me to find a wedding that's missing a bride."

"That's very bright for a cowboy," she replied. She glanced over her shoulder. "Actually . . . a wedding party has been looking for me. Think of it as a 'posse'," she added when I frowned at her. "Doesn't that make sense to you people?"

She was still trailing a veil off the crown of her head, but now she removed it.

"Sure," I told her then, "you're just about the third girl dressed like that I picked up today."

She ran the veil across my face with teasing violence so that my view was blurred a moment. Then she opened the window wide and bunched the veil up and threw it out. I watched it trail behind the car like a fleeing ghost, a soul unwinding. When I looked at her again she'd removed her shoes and pulled up her skirt as if to display her pretty legs. Not bad, too.

"Now what?" I asked.

"These are my shoes," she said, "and these are my legs."

"*Not too bad*," I told her then. "Now what are you going to do?"

"Out the window," she said and threw the shoes in the direction of the veil.

Her legs, thanks goodness, remained behind.

"Looks like I'm just in time for the honeymoon."

"Bull!" She was being pixieish, I hoped. Never liked profanity from a woman. "These happen to be perfect calves. I'm a professional."

"Then you shouldn't be wearing white," I advised her.

"Professional dancer," she explained.

Huffy little tuffy.

"Cowboys like fat calves," I told her.

"Cowgirls get the blues, you mean," she said. "They're not *that* big!"

"Bigger than mine."

"You look like you got a big one, too," she countered. "As if that mattered anyhow. Look, do we really want to talk about your legs?"

"One of us does."

Smarts. I'd panned for gold in Chiapas, Mexico, and blown the rapids on the Colorado River. Even so, nothing astonished me more than a pretty woman.

Trouble was she got up then and leaned way over her seat and reached for something in the back. Through the rear view mirror I saw plenty of nice round fanny. *"Now what?"*

"Behave, cowboy."

Over CB Cletus demanded to know who was "the seat cover?"

"Ain't no seat cover," I explained. "It's someone's wife. Ha."

"But she's wearing a wedding dress."

"Sort of."

Just then the wedding dress was also stuffed through the window. It floated out among the trees along the roadway like ectoplasm.

"Now what may she be wearing?" Cletus demanded into his microphone.

"I think she's slipping into something more comfortable," I explained. Then she turned around in short shorts and a jersey, a real cute little package. One hand went up to her eyes, and another pointed at my speedometer. Very hyper, her voice demanded, "Does that say a hundred and ten?"

I nodded.

She was about to take sick, I thought, so I eased up a little, the arrow descended, and she breathed easy and settled into her place.

"Why do you have a cowboy hat on? Never mind," she said. "How did I look in my bridal dress? Never mind that, too. I'm just a little confused. I'm 28 years old. I'm pretty. I was in town to dance at an industrial show. They had me standing inside this big white gazebo at a shopping mall with one of those old fashioned stand up mikes, and this rube dressed as a clown made jokes about my legs and showed me how to work a portable electric pencil sharpener.

"I tell you it was fairly disgusting," she went on. "I felt real crazy standing there with men staring at me like that, for no reason, among the machines. I wasn't some damn machine. They say I'm the new Edith Piaf. I performed once at the Top Of The Mark in San Francisco."

"Who was the mark who arranged that one for you?" I asked.

"Very funny. Very cute. Very clever. What did you say you do?"

"I didn't," I said. "Go on."

"It was good bread, San Francisco," she said. "I'm a good dancer. Then I got this infection . . . I won't go into any of the details . . . but I had to stop until it all cleared up. Which it has," she told me.

"Nice," I said.

"I'm alright now," she said. "But I was tired. I decided to do industrials for awhile. I didn't know I'd end up talking inside a gazebo to a clown and a talking collie dog. Anyway, after opening night I met a delicious-looking guy. Texan. He courted me right out of that gazebo and into his arms, as it were, and I thought I'd marry him and get out of the limelight awhile."

"You're making me stark raving jealous," I said.

"He was a beautiful guy," she said, "with a 28-inch waist. When I got half way down the aisle, I turned around, ran back up to the road, and broke down. Then I got into this . . . goddamn airplane. What do you do?"

"I don't remember."

"You think I'm nuts?" she asked timidly.

"Absolutely no," I said. "In fact, the bride I picked up yesterday was a singer."

She looked under her seat and found her bridal bouquet which she'd discarded upon first coming aboard. Now that she had it again she opened the window and threw it out to join her veil and dress. It scattered in the winds, more or less willy-nilly.

"This is sad," she said, very teary. "Do you hate sentiment? I hate sentiment. Do you even know what sentiment is?" she asked, or more or less demanded in fact.

Over CB, I heard Cletus, as though accompanied by the scraping fiddle music on his tape deck, declare, "Never fails. Bandit gets the chick, and I get Fred."

"Shucks," I told him.

She blushed and asked, "What's your real name?"

"Bo."

"As in 'Diddley.' "

"As in Burle M. . . . What's your name?"

She was slightly more subdued. "Carrie."

"As in carry on . . . and *on* . . . and *on* . . ."

"Shucks," she echoed me.

Welcome to my Blue Heaven. Cletus' fiddle music played "Bonaparte's Retreat." A lady who can hold her own with her mouth with a guy when he's really poking it to her. You've come a long way, baby. But every cloud that has its silver lining also has a number of large soup stains.

Right at that very moment a couple of local teenagers were popping the hubcaps off Carrie's brand new Camaro where she had abandoned it. They had just about gotten the second one loose when this 6'2" redundant Marlboro man in a Smokie hat and a tux, who happened to be Carrie's abandoned groom, wandered by with his dad, the sheriff, Buford T. Justice.

The groom, believe it or not, was called Junior, and he

was the same Junior you've already read about, except that he eventually got shrunk by grief and the hen-pecking of his dad, who stepped out of his car and immediately slapped each of the local hoods across the face. He wanted information as to the whereabouts of Carrie and he wasn't going to read them their rights before getting to work. As the late J. Edgar Hoover used to say, everybody's guilty of something or other. Treat every man according to his just deserts and who shall escape whipping?

The kids told Buford they'd seen Carrie hop into my late model Trans-Am, and they even gave him my license plate number: BAN dash ONE.

Then he tells both of them, "You don't go home, you don't eat, you don't play with yourself on my highway." They were to stay and keep watch on Carrie's car and not steal anything while he and Junior gave us chase, as it says in the old books.

So the moral to that story was, if you're gonna run out on your own wedding, don't be getting married to the deputy sheriff; but I didn't really know that yet. In my own way, I was still trying to make time with my pretty new passenger.

We were taking the hills in Mexican overdrive, but speeding up again on the inclines. Creep-and-crawl country uphill, which I converted to a buck and wing on the downslides.

Carrie asked, "Why so fast? You got some big bowling date?"

"Cute."

"At least I'm not what you would call quaint," she said.

"Quaint? No you're not," I had to admit.

She said, "So tell me about yourself."

"Okay." But I had nothing to say.

"Well?" she demanded.

"What do you want to know?" I demanded. "My sign?"

"What do you think about beside driving fast?"

"Having fun," I said. "So what else is new?"

"Is this fun?"

"Driving?"

"Driving, talking to me."

"Would you believe challenge?" I asked her.

"Challenge?"

"Challenge," I insisted. "Like chasing strange . . ."

She said, "You have a great profile."

"Only from the side," I said.

"You mean we finally agree on something?"

"Only that we both like half my face," I said.

She laughed, more like a tease than a big ha-ha.

Parked off to the side of the road, behind an abandoned and boarded-over diner, was an Arkansas State patrol car. A Smokie with a crew cut was by the side of the road taking care of his business.

I guess the whole damn force had bladder and kidney problems that week, because when we blew past at 110 he, too, tried to zip up and get on after us, only to create a big mess on the way.

Watching the whole thing, Carrie told me, "Would you be interested in a cop taking a leak at the side of the road?"

"Not enough to dance with him," I told her.

Wet hands and all, that fellow grabbed his wheel and followed on after us. Carrie said, "*Smokey*?"

I glanced in my rearview.

Sure enough . . .

I slid broadside on a 180-degree turn and went scooting up an unpaved dirt track. Locking all four tires, I sent the Trans-Am into a four-wheel drift.

As I'm doing all this I'm singing to myself a little ditty from God knows when, my childhood or younger days maybe:

"Takes a heap of man
To say glad I can.
Takes a lot of pride
in what I am . . .
Takes a lot of pressed pork
to make one can of Spam. . . ."

Carrie said, "What's happening? Am I alive or dead?"

"Ladies and gentlemen," I said into the CB, but also for her benefit, "fasten your safety belts."

We slid like greasy pellets in a bearing track. Carrie asked, "Is this fun?"

But she buckled up. Then I told Snowman, "Got your ears on, big fella? Because I'm gonna leave you for a minute."

"Keep her between the ditches . . . and the bitches without their britches," he replied, making Carrie blush.

I stepped on it and we roared on down the dirt, making clouds like Hiroshima in our wake. That Smokie followed us in hot pursuit.

Carrie asked, "*This* is fun, *for sure*?"

"You better believe," I told her, "it ain't no grab ass. I forgot to tell you—I'm running blocker for 400 cases of illegal brew."

"Gotcha!" She didn't really understand, but what could she do under the circumstances?

With solid dust between me and that patrol car I couldn't see a thing behind me, and not too much up front either. When I turned on my wipers the dust was twice as thick.

I slid into another quick right turn and stopped short. The Smokey missed the turn, sailed on down the road, took off out of control, and flew right into a water hole, sinking all the way up to his windows.

Carrie said, "What now?"

I answered her by taking off again down that dirt road.

"Holy shit!" she swore.

"That and more," I told her.

Over CB Cletus was yammering: "Bandit I. Bandit I. Do you read me?"

"Snowman give us another thin mint and we'll be back on the long brown chocolate." That was our way of saying one minute to the highway, in case we were being monitored, which I should also mention we were at that very moment by Sheriff Justice and Carrie's disappointed bridegroom, Junior.

Cletus said, "I'll keep my eyeballs peeled."

"And your pedal floored," I told him.

Meanwhile, far back on the same highway, Buford T. Justice, sheriff, was orating to his son with the CB radio button down: "Nobody walks out on a weddin' with my boy. We gonna get that girl and set everything back straight."

"Maybe," Junior said.

"Shut up. She insulted me, my son."

"Maybe."

"Shut up. She insulted my authority. She insulted a sheriff of Texarkana. That's old fashioned Communism, comes from dancers hanging out with all them *fags*. Right?"

"Maybe."

Justice said, "Don't leave *me* at no church."

"Don't dress up my town for no reason," Justice said.

"Running back up the aisle," Justice said. "Worse than that—dancin' back up the aisle."

"Maybe."

"No maybe," he said. "That was dancin'." He was so furious you'd have thought he'd personally been jilted.

After a while I switched back to Cletus' channel: "Snowman, have you copied the Smokey talkie?"

"This is Snowman," he said. I could hear Fred snoring over the filter mike. "Now where the hell are you?"

"On two lane blacktop. Mile marker six-one. How we doin' on time?"

"Twenty-eight minutes ahead of schedule," Cletus insisted.

"What's your twenty?" I asked.

"I'm about four miles ahead of you, turkey."

"Not for long, you ain't," I said.

Suddenly, a familiar-sounding voice interrupted us: "Breaker. Breaker."

"Go breaker," I said.

"I got a Smokey report for you."

"Go head on, breaker."

"You got trouble comin'."

"What's your handle, and what's your twenty?"

"My handle's Smokey Bear, and my twenty's on your ass, and I'm gonna sass you, Bandit."

A siren blasted us in our seats. Peering back through the rear view mirror, I saw this Smokey with Texas plates just about to tailgate me and trounced it hard, laying 20 feet of third-gear rubber. That Texas sheriff's car suddenly looked like it was standing up on jacks.

"That's a Texas cop," I told Carrie. "What in the hell's he doing in Arkansas?"

"I don't know," she said, grimly. "I . . . don't

know. I don't know. Maybe it comes from all that chasing strange . . ."

I was doing 120 easy. When Carrie reached for her cigarettes, they flew backwards out of her pack. She was coughing furiously when she finally lit up. That Smokey tried to stay on my tail, but it had lost a little distance as we approached Cletus in Bandit II.

I swung around him then and flicked on my CB. "I'm end-running you Snowman. Smokey on the rubber *hubba dubba*."

Snowman saw traffic coming head-on as I tried to pass and told me so. "Hold back. You gotta make your own lane, buddy. You got oncoming."

I turned to face Carrie a moment and then I floored it. At first she shrugged, and then she stared ahead, her body rigid, only her mouth moving: "Well *gollee bum* . . . *gollee* . . . I've had a good life . . . I have never wronged another person . . . I wouldn't hurt you and I hope you won't hurt me. *Gollee bum* . . . you're going very fast, although, of course, I don't like to criticize. . . ." She squeezed her eyes and a tear crept out. "I want to live . . . Ohhhhhh . . . *Gollee bum*." She closed her eyes.

We were steaming along, seeming A-O.K. When she opened her eyes to the clear highway, Carrie said, "You're a very good driver and a good person. . . . Don't kill me. . . . Say . . . say . . . say something."

"Everything will be alright," I told her as I flew off the highway onto the shoulder to avoid that sudden oncoming, and skittered and flailed and kept right on with Carrie's eyes tight shut again.

Driving, I heard her scream, "OOHHHHHHHHHHHHH-HHHHHHHHHH!" Like she was getting off hard and scared.

"Where you fixin' to go?" she asked, as I pulled abreast of Snowman's 18-wheeler from the soft shoulder, just barely hanging onto my strip of road for dear life.

Up ahead was a dirt road crossing and I thought I would never make it past Cletus in time to get over to the other side. I hit the dirt and the Trans-Am went back on two wheels and flew up into the air, comin down smash against a highway sign and sending it splintering 20 feet into the air.

"My God," went Carrie. "I hope this contraption don't fall apart."

All of a sudden there was such an endless row of mailboxes staring at me, and before I could whip the wheel around, I went right at them: *Whap! Whap! Whap! Whap!* Then I dropped the Trans-Am back into first and zoomed on past Bandit II, out onto the highway again.

"You okay?" I asked her.

"Holy shit!" she shouted. "They, Lord . . . What next?"

While from Buford's car, like a public address, I could hear him announcing to Junior, "Seem' to me we dealin' here with a total lack of respect for the law."

"Give a hissy, Daddy," says the boy. "You been fixin' to anyway . . . a long, long time."

But he was trapped behind our big 18-wheeler, and when he pulled out in an effort to squeeze between Bandit II and the oncoming, seven other cars were forced to hit the soft shoulder. A symphony of horns started up.

Just as Buford moved on halfway past again, Cletus put on the press and edged Sheriff Justice over. His rear fender caught against the rig and ripped off with a terrifying screech. As his fender bounced off alone, Justice pulled in front of Bandit II.

Cletus knew the passing car was heat, so he flipped over to the next odd channel and keyed up his CB: "Bandit I, do I have you copying?"

"Yeah, Snowman."

"That's a Texas bubble gum machine on your back porch."

Carrie repeated what she'd just heard, not understanding, "Back porch? Gum ball machine? Where?"

"I see him, Cletus," I said.

"What's a Texas County Mounty doing here in Arkansas?"

I glanced at Carrie. "You tell me baby," I asked.

"I don't know . . . I don't know . . ." she said quietly, as if fixing to hide behind her own protests.

That woman was all varnish for that moment, as I slammed down the mike and hit the go pedal once more. Now the chase was on full force, as we say down my way. Our two cars was just two big blurs along the Arkansas countryside. Up hill and down dale.

Over the blast off I heard: "Bandit, your ass is grass and I'm a gonna be the lawn mower . . . you watch. This is Sheriff Justice. In pursuit of a black Trans-Am, Georgia plates BOY ADAM NORA OCEAN NORA EDDIE. Request assistance."

That lit the game board up all over the state. Twirling lights and wailing sirens started up at once from Pine Bluffs to Hot Springs. One who pot-lucked that signal was Sheriff George Brandford and his deputy, Digby.

Brandford was black, six-foot-eight, all spit and polish, and driving. Digby resembled a wart under long sideburns and mirrored sunglasses. The twerp couldn't manage to chew his bubble gum and drive at the same time.

He got Justice on the cooker and turned the mike over to Brandford: "This is Sheriff George Brandford of Crosset County, Arkansas. We are apprised of the situation and are taking appropriate measures. Did you say you are a sheriff?"

"That's a big ten-four," says Buford, having trouble steering and talking at the same time. "This is Sheriff Texas from Justice . . . or vice versa," he added.

"*Texas?*" Brandford was, to say the least, incredulous. "You know, of course, you are way out of your jurisdiction. May I suggest that my department handle this situation?"

"Repeat. I am in high speed pursuit. Don't you hear good?"

"I hear A-O.K. The fact that you are a sheriff is not germane . . . you are still out of your jurisdiction."

"Darn Germans got nothing to do with it," said Justice, as he slammed down the mike and continued the chase.

Tallyho! I sure was a fast fox. After a bit Buford was on the tube again. "This is Justice. I lost the Trans-Am, but he's dead headed toward you doin' damn near 140. If I was you, I'd set up a roadblock."

"Sheriff," said Brandford, "I believe we have the situation well under control."

My needle was beyond 120. My whole right foot felt numb, with tiny pins and needles alternating. Just as I thought we'd lost Buford, I heard another voice over CB: "Bandit, do you read me?"

"This is Bandit, and you're coming in loud and proud."

"My handle's Silver Tongued Devil, and I'm here to tell you your fellow China Burmas are mighty proud of y'all."

"Thanks much Silver Tongued Devil."

"STD for short to you," he said. "But have I got a bad Bear story for you . . . just rolled past a County Mounty roadblock down on highway eighty-two."

"You are indeed silver tongued," I said.

He said, "Keep the wheels spinning and the beavers grinning."

"And the bears' ranks thinning," I added.

"I'm out."

"Adios," I said.

Even Carrie was impressed because she said, "Classy type guy."

Fine eye, too, because when I took the next turn at only 90 or so, we looked up and there was two County Mounties parked across the road a mile away. I threw the car into a broadside and swerved off the road, lurched my way onto a farmhouse driveway, and barreled across the front yard. A clothesline snapped against my grille, sending bras, panties, shirts, and socks flying like autumn leaves or racing flags. Well, those Arky Mounties gave chase after they got their mouths shut from amazement, and we skedaddled so fast down that narrow road toward Mulberry Bridge (to which all road signs were pointing) without any knowledge the bridge had been dismantled only last month.

Coming up on our rear were the Arky Mounties, and behind them Buford and his sonny boy, I guess. When I saw a big wet ditch with nothing going across it to the other side, I was maybe 50 yards away and I turned a 180 and saw the cavalry approaching me dead on and there was only one thing I knew how to do. I spun it again and headed straight at the ditch.

"Why don't you just drop me here?" Carrie said. "I'll get a cab."

I didn't have the time. As soon as my front wheels hit the embankment we were airborne. Gung ho. Below us the creek shimmered between immense bare white boulders. We came crashing down on our springs on the other side.

As Carrie caught her breath, I asked her, "Having fun?"

"Does the Pope wear diapers?" she replied.

Grinning, I hit the slammer again.

The Mounties came right after us. One dropped directly into the creek below, but Sheriff Brandford got caught hanging halfway over the edge, suspended, as it were, in mid-chassis.

The sheriff was hanging onto the dashboard just getting used to his precarious new situation when Buford came rushing up and slammed right into his luggage compartment, knocking him and his deputy into the drink. The splash Carrie and I heard seconds later was over CB radio, muted and bubbly, as if played on a washing machine.

She said, "You certainly aren't the type who waits around to be reproached."

"Should I be?" I asked her.

"Not for my sake," she said. "I really couldn't care less."

XVI

Quivering Quicksilver

We roared back onto the highway again from dirt track like a husband rushing home to momma in a dead heat. Carrie was calming herself by chain-smoking. I got my nerves together compiling recipes for a cookbook I hope to publish someday: The Saddlesoap Cookbook, one hundred unusual and different ways to use saddlesoap in your kitchen to make appetizing meals for your whole family. Right then I was working on saddlesoap soup . . . with pork bristles.

I guess I do this sort of thing whenever hunger grips me on the road. Everybody's got an old can of saddlesoap lying around the house and thinking of everything cooked in saddlesoap sort of controls the gnawing deep down inside. But it wasn't working this time as well as it had in the past. No doubt about it: I'd used up a whole lot of adrenaline leaping that ditch.

I punched in channel 11 and called out, "Snowman, Snowman. Give me a shout."

"I'm here and I'm working," Cletus said. "This is my month. What have you been doing—dipping your stinger in honey?"

"Where do we stand?" I asked, as I caught sight of his 18 wheels ahead of me.

"We're losing minutes," Cletus said, "so you better start running interference or we're never gonna make it."

"I'll drop off my fare, hit a quick choke and puke, and be blocking for you pronto," I said.

I could see Carrie was trying not to show any interest, but I was still much too busy with Cletus.

"Bandit?"

"Yeah, guy?"

"Pick up a burger for Fred. He's eating my shoes."

"Ten-four." I switched off.

"Choke and puke is a diner," I told her. "In case you didn't know."

"Where I come from, we call it hit and run," she said.

"Not bad."

"It is if you have to run," she said, "or get them. Is that where I get let off?"

"Right." It wasn't all I wanted to do, but I would do just that anyway. Who had time for anything else?

A few minutes later the CHOMP STOP DINER came up on my right, sky blue and crowded in front with 18-wheelers. I pulled in between the heavies to a complete stop.

"Here we are, Miss. . . . Er, you got enough bread for a ticket?"

"Enough to get me to Jersey," she said. "If necessary I'll walk the rest of the way. Well," she added, "it's been a trip."

"Hey, you going to be alright?"

"Sure enough . . . Nice meeting you."

"Keep your thumb up and your skirts down," I said.

"Keep your nose to the wheel *schlemiel*," she slammed right back at me.

That stopped me a second or more. But my stomach was beginning to ache so I headed toward the diner. She started off toward the bus stop. Halfway up the stoop I turned to look back, but she kept on going.

Inside was convention time. Trucking friends of the road everywhere, and the intoxicating smell of burning grease, hot java, and fried onions. It didn't take me too long to get a big sack of food made up for all of us, and I was moving away from the counter when I bumped right into this Mounty, spilling coffee and mustard all over the front of his entire uniform.

I'll have to add that one to my saddlesoap recipes, I thought, as I excused myself and reached for some soapy napkins to mop up the mess as it dripped down beneath the sheriff's front buttons.

"Easy boy," he told me. "You got no eyes."

I'd have recognized that foghorn anywhere. Sheriff Buford. All I could do was be cool and kind.

"I'm sorry, Sheriff. This really was my fault."

"Course it was," he told me. "Weren't mine." As he walked, I continued dabbing and wiping. We came to the end of the counter and he clawed one of those cellophane-wrapped, ready-made sandwiches and took a big bite.

With a mouthful, he called out, "Two coffees to go. Make it quick." All that cellophane made him sound a bit like he was blowing on a combophone.

I said, "Man, you gotta be in some kind of hurry."

"You can bet your ass on that, boy!"

He took another bite and crackled more cellophane. "I've been chasing a goddamn mental case. All the way from Texas."

"Texas? What did he do? Rob a bank?" I took another stab at his chest with the napkin, leaving behind a hunk of lint.

"That's enough of that," he told me then. "Robbin' a bank's baby-stuff for sure alongside what he's done. This sumbitchin' maniac near killed ten troopers. He's driven through people's backyards, knocked down a whole row of mailboxes. He's got a girl in the car he's driven across a state line . . . against the girl's will. That's kidnappin'. How's that for hijinks!"

He popped the last bite of his sandwich in his mouth and blew out a large bubble of cellophane; then he asked the waitress, "What do I owe you, nice lady?"

I said it was on me.

He didn't say thanks right away. Just asked me where the can was. Seemed he had to make a quick stop.

"Back there, sir," I told him.

He patted my shoulder and belched again. "You're a good old boy."

I went outside just in time to see my Trans-Am doing a slow 180-degree turn. It was headed in the direction of Texarkana, the wrong direction. I ran down the steps and raced toward the car just as it was peeling off toward the out ramp. I swung open the passenger door and was half in, half out, before I saw it was Carrie behind the wheel as the Trans-Am bumped the curb and teetered toward the highway. The door hung open, and I was still hanging on. Carrie stomped on the pedal and the car took off like greased lightning. I just about stayed half in the car.

"What the hell are you doing?" I demanded, still hanging on.

She gestured over her shoulder. "He's after us again."

"That's terrific," I told her, "but you're going the wrong way."

She slammed on the brakes and hung a neat, complete U-turn in the middle of the road.

I said, "Let's go, sweety," hanging on all the while.

Junior came rushing out of the diner and tried to stop us with his body. Carrie narrowly missed him.

"Watch your ass, Fiance," she shouted.

I crawled inside and we sped off with Carrie still doing pin turns this way and that.

"Look," she told me, "the truth is I didn't want to be dumped at the truck stop. I wanted to go on with you but I needed an excuse."

"Couldn't you ask?"

"You might have said no," she told me. "I always have trouble handling rejection."

We were getting somewhere together, even though we still had Junior and Buford tailing us. One minute I looked and they were driving a sedan. But then they ducked at the very last minute beneath this enormous rig bearing a crane and came out driving a convertible. Still they kept on coming on.

Carrie drove like she took lessons from me; turns at 85 and better than 100 on the straightaways. A prodigy for sure. She had me holding on by the safety straps.

"Please don't do that anymore," I told her, when she went around one corner at 100 with her other foot nowhere near the brake pedal.

"It does look different from over there," Carrie said, "don't it?"

I picked up the mike and flicked the crystal selector two stops down.

"Breaker, this is Bandit I, how are your vocal cords?"

"My vocal cords are fine," said Cletus, "but Fred's ain't. He's been barking, eating the seats, driving me crackers, and now he's doing something dirty in my lap."

I heard barking.

"What's your twenty now?" I asked.

" 'Bout 14 miles this side of Mississippi," he said.

Cletus was way ahead of me again. He told me he was slowing down to 55 because he had just spotted two Kojaks with a Kodak.

Radar. I had Carrie hang back a little.

After a while I heard Cletus ask, "Where the hell are you? Man, this highway's crawling with Bears."

I looked back over my shoulder and it was likewise I'm sure with me, too.

"Golly buddy," I told him, "I'm still trying to ditch this Texas Smokey. I don't know what the sucker wants."

"Probably what they all want," went Cletus, "to handcuff a legend."

Well if that's what he really wanted, I was bound to give him a fair try on an offside kick. I told Carrie to plan on changing seats and over CB advised Cletus to give me five minutes to ditch my idiot and then I would meet him "in Ole Miss."

"Kiss that money good-bye if you don't" he signed off.

There was a funeral procession making a left turn on the highway, and Carrie got between two limos and wheeled her way down a side street. I climbed up on the seat divider and tried to get her to change places, but our legs got all tangled and there wasn't very much room. The car hit a 360-degree spin and was heading backwards down a dirt road.

"Close," I told her, as I tried it again and failed, and she hung a right in a cornfield and moved her way through acres of dry-old husks.

Thanks to the Lord, poor old Buford had to wait out that

whole funeral procession, because I let her stay behind the wheel, and we took every bump and every furrow

Carrie was motor-mouthing all the while: "You know I used to be a high fashion model. Tried it for six months and almost freaked. Makeup, silly clothes. You know it's tough when your cheekbones are your main asset."

"They sure are," I grinned.

"People say a girl like me is probably pretty loose from being photographed and looked at all the time, but I'm telling you it don't work that way."

"Like what?"

"If I'm not interested, I just don't," Carrie said, and then, Whoa there . . . Whoa . . ."

Too late! Up ahead of us 20 yards, the path ended on an incline and beyond that was a fence. She got her feet confused and we went charging right through the fence and into this bare field where a little league football game was in progress. All the kids were running and screaming and the coach looked flabbergasted. Carrie straightened out and tore off across the field. In the middle she did a 360-degree fishtail and, with players scattering in every direction, drove past the dugout and the cheering crowd back up to an access road.

"Gear down," I said, but she went just the other way and zoomed.

After a while we were back on the highway again. Carrie grinned at me. "You've done a lot for the sport," I told her, grinning back more easily.

The big muddy Mississippi river is as wide as an inland sea about where we crossed on an old bridge. Below us the turbid waters lapped against cantilevers, and barges proceeded slowly far off, like big cakes of industrial soap floating in a tub. I thought of Huck Finn and Jim floating down this same wet roadway over 100 years ago. One thing Mark Twain had right about travel in this country: it helps to have company by your side.

As we came abreast of the distant shoreline, I told Carrie, "Spectacular view . . . Indians called it the water snake with many tongues."

"Nice," she cooed. "Nice."

We entered Mississippi like day-old bread popping out of the toaster. As soon as we were in a new state I got on the jammer again to Cletus and asked him for another twenty.

"I'm at marker 85," he told me, "that's 8-5."

"Son of a gun," I said, "me too."

It was seconds later that I saw his big rig chugging along. We came alongside and he pulled over to the shoulder, stopped, and dismounted. I pulled on ahead and got out with Carrie. Carrie introduced herself to Cletus who was taking big long stretches. Then I had her feed a sandwich to Fred who wolfed it all down in one big gulp, while Cletus took me by the arm and pulled me off to one side. He'd thought I was dumping the chick at the truck stop and didn't seem to want to understand about the complications.

"You know," he said, "every time we've ever messed up it's because you've let your alligator mouth overload your jaybird ass. I know you think you're God's gift to waitresses, but . . ."

"How we doing time-wise?" I interrupted him.

"Not good."

I turned to leave. "We're gone."

"Bandit?" he called me, and as I turned he winked. "Nice ass."

"Nice meeting you Cletus," Carrie said, as I dragged her back to the car and we took off. "Keep on truckin'!"

He had some trouble rounding up old Fred again, but when we were all together and high-tailing along, a silence fell between Carrie and me.

Finally she broke it. "Why did Cletus call you a legend back there?"

"I used to do a lot of crazy things," I told her.

"And not anymore, of course."

"Of course."

She nodded and so did I. It was still all a mystery to her.

We drove a straight line toward Winona with Carrie chattering most of the time. I can't even remember all she asked me. Mostly it was just questions. How old was I? How old was Cletus? Did he have a wife and kiddies? Did I have a wife and kiddies? A family? Pay income taxes? Support the ERA? Was I Protestant? Catholic? Jewish? And if the former, from what exact sect? Did I care to know to what sect she belonged? Had I ever been married? Was I a veteran? Did I believe in free choice for women? Would I care to know more about her personal history? So on and so forth.

One point she became real specific. "A gypsy," she told me, "is a dancer in a chorus line who just keeps moving from show to show . . . so what's your excuse? Why do you keep moving?"

"Well, if you keep moving, they say . . ." I was trying hard to fake it.

"Just this once don't pull my leg," Carrie said. She looked at me sternly. I felt her look and it was serious between us.

"Okay. I keep moving because . . . I don't know . . ." (I really didn't). "It feels like . . ." (I made a motion with my hands which took them off the wheel and the car veered, so I had to place them back on again). "Sure ain't no money in it," I went on, as if thinking aloud. But I really couldn't find the right words, the right excuses. I knew she wouldn't settle for more of my bull. I felt her tender pleading glances. "It's like I needed . . ."

"Prestige?" she asked, as if she could read my mind.

It wasn't only that, but I nodded to make things easier between us. "Yeah . . . prestige . . . maybe that's it."

"Go on," she said with a nod, as if she was my shrink.

"Hell, I never talked about my life." Being serious made me feel so uncomfortable. I'm nobody's fool, but I really don't like to take myself that seriously.

"Go on," Carrie insisted softly, as if she really cared to know. To know for sure, it seemed.

"What I do," I said, "whatever it is . . . I like it." I really couldn't say it any better than that.

Carrie remained silent. She was staring straight ahead. But when I looked over at her, I could see there were tears in her eyes. Some women really move a man and that's all there is to it: and others just don't.

I didn't like feeling so uncomfortable with the possibility of my own tears, so I did my Gabby Hayes bit: "Let's move it. This wagon train's got to roll all the way to Atlanta."

XVII

Open Country Jamming

"Across the open countryside and into the arms of my baby I ride" is an old motorcycling song of my youth when us boys in our leather jackets on the big hogs took off going nowhere very fast indeed. But, as it felt now like I had my baby with me in the next seat, I tried to banish all such thoughts from my mind and let the good feeling just sit there inside my body. It's a blessing when you can feel tears or that you want to break down and cry, as long as you can control it.

So we zoomed, but with as much caution as possible. No more Smokies for me if they could be avoided. I thought of nothing but the landscape blurring alongside our windows and Carrie and me playing house quietly inside my cockpit. But just beyond Eupora I saw a light green, late model Merc sedan with a radio antenna coming at us as if to eat us with its grille. I tbought to myself SMOKEY and took my foot off the hopper.

"Foot fall asleep?" Carrie asked, as if stirred suddenly out of her own little nod.

I shook my head and reached for the CB. "Snowman, Smokey in a plain brown wrapper pointing your way."

No answer from Cletus.

Carrie said, "That must mean an unmarked police vehicle?"

"Very good. You get an A for that one, luv." But I was worried about Cletus and on the mike again. "Snowman, bring yourself on in."

Zeros again. Snake eyes.

"Is you is or is you ain't my Snowman?" I whined and wheedled, imagining all kinds of game plans: he'd run off the road, been hooked by Smokies, or Fred was taking a leak and Cletus couldn't drag him back into the cab of the truck.

Turned out the latter was the problem, and after I hollered again, "Snowman, with your coal black eyes and carrot nose, are you there?", his words sang in my ears: "Yeah, yeah, yeah? What's shaking, Bandit?"

"When you get everything straightened out," I advised, "put the hammer down and look out for a big Smokey frown bearing down."

"Got ya! Ten-four, barring my door." He must have started up his rig, checked for oncoming, and pulled out onto the highway again.

After another little while I heard him say, "Bandit, you read my mind like the Sunday comics. I am right behind you."

When I looked, there he was, a law-abiding trucker hauling commerces, half a mile to my rear, with his dog in the next seat.

Hauling my ashes was more or less what was on my mind, but I kept that pretty much to myself. With a woman like Carrie, plain and simple gross vulgarity is bound to be a loser. Licentious buffoonery is on the way out, and so is seductiveness. She moved my heart; I knew it and she knew it, too. Best thing to do was take care of this business now and that business later. Now I would tell her of the battles I had fought.

Out through Matheston and Maben I found myself explaining about my unhappy childhood and erratic adolescence in more or less clinical terms, as if I wanted her to understand it wasn't all my fault and I wasn't all that bad. Mostly, I just kept right on pouring it on, mile after mile after mile, gallon after gallon. Sometimes I counted in miles and sometimes in kilometers (as there were those new markers along some parts of the road), whichever seemed the shorter to my mind.

My kidneys were aching after a while, and we were also running out of engine firewater, so I got on the jammer again and told Snowman I had to make a quick pit stop.

"Whatever for?" he jibed. "Now what?"

"Running out of motion lotion."

"So I'll keep on streaking," he said, "and peaking on ahead. Pick me up. Later."

As Bandit II went sailing down the highway, I took the off ramp. There was a big Union 76 station waiting just below the underpass for us, and I pulled up to one of the islands.

"Kidney tapping time," I said.

"Save my seat for me," Carrie said.

"In the ladies' you'll be on your own," I quipped and instantly felt real bad. Lousy. For talking dirty with her again like that. It was like lying to a woman, unnecessary if you're really prepared to communicate, and I noticed she was frowning a little as she strutted off toward the head.

"Trans-Am, what would be your pleasure?" asked the young black attendant of me then. "I recommend the oil but the gas is pretty good, too, if you're into high octane."

Moody still, I said, "Funny fellow."

"Hey," he jived back, "this is one clean machine. Ya—I was thinking about getting one of these myself. But I figure I'm conspicuous enough as it is. What's happening?"

"Everything," I told him.

He must have been a college student in his free time, because then he started jiving me real fancy: "Don't you think that's right on? About me being conspicuous, I mean. You wouldn't confuse me for David Bowie? Am I right, or right?"

"Right you are," I said. "Nor Willie Nelson for that matter."

"Nor Cheryl Tiegs?"

"She's a girl," I said. "Now how about some gas?"

"Fill it, my man?"

"Please." But so he wouldn't feel too badly, I added, "Man delights not me. Nor women either."

"Sounds good to me," said Joe College, pumping me full of Supreme.

I listened to those gurgling bongs and watched the little black numbers mount up.

Suddenly over CB a voice came loud and clear: "BANDIT DO YOU READ ME?"

"I was startled. I grabbed the mike. "This is Bandit. Who we got on that end?"

As if I didn't know. "You got the man what's gonna put you in the slammer—Sheriff Buford Justice of Texarkana, Texas."

"Well, Sheriff Justice," I said, "welcome to Mississippi."

"Thank you kindly." He seemed to forget himself a moment. But then. "Damn you, boy, don't you sass me on this here radio."

"Then don't swear at me on this here radio."

"I apologize to everyone who's listening."

I thought for a minute he said he apologized for living, and it sounded just thc way ma used to sound when she was sick, and lonely, and reproachful because I didn't call sometimes, but then he added, just like ma when she was being disagreeable, "You'll be sorry for the day you were born . . . you sorry son of a bitch," only she wouldn't ever call me that because where would that leave her as a mother?

Justice added, "I've come this far . . ."

"I've been meaning to ask about that, Sheriff," I interrupted. "Why are you following me?"

Justice sounded real intense, a conspiracy of one: "Boy, I'm not following you. I am tracking you down. I am bringing you in. . . . THERE'S SOMETHING THE MATTER WITH YOU BOY," he added in a tone that made you think he was weeping. "I GOTTA TAKE YOU IN FOR THE PROTECTION OF THE CITIZENRY. YOU ARE A PUBLIC NUISANCE . . . A VERITABLE MADMAN . . . YOU HAVE NO RESPECT . . . NO RESPECT FOR LAW AND ORDER."

"Order me a ham on rye," I said. "Sheriff?"

"What is it, young man?"

"Do the letters F.O. mean anything to you?"

I was greeted with a guttural, incoherent babble, so I

hung up the mike again as Carrie reappeared, sipping at an orange sodey. She hopped into the front seat with her Nehi as the attendant strutted over with change from a fifty for my Union Koolaid.

He flashed me five and slapped my palm with greenbacks, one by one, and said, "Have a smooth one, Mr. Bandit."

"So you knew all the time?"

"Like why not?" said he. "It's cool with me no matter what you do . . . so long as you don't run over my sister in the street."

I nodded, threw the Trans-Am into gear, and took off like a Phantom jet. As I rounded the service area and the grease pit, I sailed right on past Sheriff Justice's squad car. All this time we'd been maybe 50 feet away from one another transmitting.

Roaring out onto the blacktop, I saw the sheriff whip his head around, absolutely stunned, and I stopped a split second to watch the fun. Justice ran to his car and started up the engine and really stomped on it. Unfortunately, the front end was pumped up on jacks, so his car just took off on its rear wheels, sailing halfway across the gas station and slamming head-on into a brand-new Lincoln Continental. That Continental sails like a billiard on green felt across all the islands and against a nearby stanchion with a big dent in its shiny new coat of paint.

Poor Buford watched all this with mounting horror, as if he could not quite believe the evidence of his own incompetence. Then I took off like greased lightning, but I could still hear him talking to himself over the CB: "It's alright. It's not your car. You're doing fine. Keep going."

Then the crazy coot actually started broadcasting: "Attention all cars. This is Sheriff Buford T. Justice from Texas. That Trans-Am y'all been lookin' for is now southbound on Interstate 82. Heading for Alabama."

A thick-drawling Mississippian interrupted: "That's a big ten-four, Texas. Now we gonna nail that joy ridin' CB freak-frak sumbitch."

But by then I was eating up blacktop, even passing

Snowman again in Bandit II. Leaving the straight life behind, as Bobby Goldsboro says.

I told Cletus, "Looks to me like a clear shot to the 'Bama state line."

"I'll believe it when I see it," he told me.

It's right about then I began to feel like I was in some kind of moving picture or TV show or something. I mean, here I am with a beautiful frail next to my elbow in this clean and sharp Tans-Am, cruising along at the speed of sound, with my oldest good buddy right behind me in an 18-wheeler. I swear it felt like we should have been taking pictures of ourselves, we looked so beautiful—so good. So clean and free and easy . . . a Peter Fonda flick from the 60s maybe, or that Technicolor movie with Al Pacino about car driving.

The best life is behind the wheel, let me tell you, unless you're on the horizontal with someone you like a whole lot. I get my very best thoughts on the road. Like I began thinking of this writer feller Jack Kerouac, a beatnik. They say he drank himself to death. That's because he traveled so light with his thumb, instead of in a Trans-Am. Never had a plug dollar in his pockets and no pride as a man. Too close to his mother . . . I guess that's sad. A man needs to feel he can get off without even trying, and that's what your Trans-Am is all about when you've got a pretty lady by your side. Going down country roads and bringing home the side pork and bacon to suit yourself is what it's all about. I felt right then and there, after my first few episodes with Carrie, that we oughta be in pictures together. Something a lot more important than just country roads was happening between us.

Driving through the wild and woolly forest parts of Mississippi, the brush as thick as Dolly Parton's hairdo, I thought to myself we better get us to 'Bama fast or we would get jumped from behind a hedgerow or thicket. Finally, we came out in clear country again about 200 miles east of Big Muddy and there, beside a creek, were three patrol cars from Ole Miss. Their pinwheels were lit up and swirling, and they were parked to form a solid roadblock next to an old 7-11 store; I could see from a quarter of a mile off they were waiting for Bandit. For a split second I thought about this good old boy I knew down in Citronelle and how maybe I just ought to veer straight south and hit him with an impromptu visitation, but, of course, there was the time factor to worry about, so I let my reflexes do the taking over.

"You ready?" I asked Carrie.

"Bandit," she told me, "I was born ready."

Bye bye Citronelle and hello Alexander City and parts east. I swerved the wheel to the right and made a big sliding turn off the highway.

"Now what?" Carrie asked.

"Just studying the situation," I explained.

Two of those patrol cars were forming up a roadblock. As I approached at close to top speed, penetrating to the other side seemed impossible. They had me by the shorties. I broadsided the car and stopped dead in the middle of the highway, my motor fluttering. It was the only noise which could be heard.

An elderly couple came out to the porch of the 7-11, as if they was watching General Sherman's army about to parade by.

I saw the first patrol car start to roll and that was the break I wanted. He had committed himself going one way, so I backed off the road and swung around fast, circling the roadblock, and out behind the out building to where the highway was clear as spring water again.

"Get that sumbitch," said the first trooper, who looked like a sergeant.

He and his flunky dove for their cars, the sergeant second in formation behind the trooper. Well, that trooper must have got his gears jammed, because instead of going forward, he backed up and knocked the sergeant straight backwards in his car into the nearby stream and disabled his own car in the process.

Now I had only the third patrol car to worry about and it was swinging wide around the 7-11 to come on after me. We went up a winding mountain road alongside the stream and there were men in hip waders fishing among the rapids. They waved at me in the misty air with their rods, like leprechauns and fairies handling magic wands. Make him go away if you really care, Mr. God, I thought to myself as we careened together, one behind the next, down the other side of this same mountain creek road.

Then I asked Carrie, "Do you swim?"

"Why?" she asked, looking serious and slightly worried again, the pallor on her face like heavy powder.

"You'll learn," I told her then, "if it comes to that."

I hung a sharp right and almost flew off the road into the stream and across, like an LST at Inchon, Korea. Splat went our wheels, and skidder-didder-dadder went the jammers when I hit them hard and squeezed, as we disappeared up a small path into some woods.

The trooper came reeling over the embankment after me and did a bellyflop splashdown into the stream. He tried to take off after me again, but skittered and diddered, hit a rock, went broadside, and slid right back into deep water. Struck in the muck, hip deep in the Little Muddy.

The woods we drove through then were lovely, dark and deep. A light fog gently enveloped our car, its soft gray wetness a miniature rain. We seemed almost invisible in the forest. Deer came to the windows and fed out of Carrie's little hand on small pieces of sandwich bread as we drove slowly along an old logging trail which eventually led us to the main highway some five or six miles down the way.

Then we started climbing, taking every turn fast, making time, much faster than ever, as we passed all those fancy metal signs reading CURVES AHEAD, SLIPPERY WHEN WET, SLOW, DEER CROSSING, SCHOOL CHILDREN, FALLING ROCK ZONE. Finally, we reached the end of Mississippi and crossed the border into Alabama, where we caught up with Bandit II again, keeping the pace, smoke-stacks blasting. I gave him a toot to the front end as we passed, happy as cooties. Beautiful nature is a wonderful thing when a man and a woman are riding through it together.

Despite all that, Buford remained on our tails, and we couldn't quite shake him. His car was disintegrating, but his will was like beveled steel. He came by that 7-11 store just when the state tow truck arrived to pull those troopers and their cars out of the drink. Buford's front end was now totaled and his top was gone, like somebody'd ripped it off with a key from a can of sardines.

Leaving his side door open to the road, he came out and went over to talk to the tow truck driver about who was responsible for all this devastation. As if he couldn't bring himself to guess.

Couple on the porch says, "Got some fresh country scrapple if you're hungry, Sheriff."

"Hot damn," says he.

"*Does that mean yes or no?*" asks the old guy.

"It means I'm chasing varmints," said Buford, "and never interrupt the line of duty for mere bodily needs."

"Noble are the brave," says the old lady then. "The stars and bars . . . may they wave forever."

"Indeed. Indeed," went Buford, as he ascertained that a fellow name of Bandit was the cause of all these new piles of scrap iron.

He was heading back toward what was left of his sedan when this giant 18-wheeler hauling a wide load of split pine came barreling down the highway.

"Watch yourself, bud," cried Buford.

Too late. His side door was ripped right off its hinges and sent soaring 30 feet into the air. Some fellas are just damn hard on their vehicles is all, I guess; no doubt about it.

XVIII

The Kindness of Lovers and Other Strangers

Carrie was dozing when I grabbed the shoulder down through 'Bamaland, hugging every curve; so it was just as well her eyes were closed. A certain slant of light was in our eyes; I squinted as I drove, and the car's engine roared as if we were speeding out of the throat of an enormous metal bullhorn.

In the old days I always took this road to Selma when the sit-ins were in session, and I had a couple of friends in the black truckers association. We would get together and bring in tents and field rations for the marchers. Those were desperate but good times. A man felt like he made a difference in the world then, but it had been years since I'd been down anywhere near this part of the country and I was a different man now, and so was Alabama. Some black people were making it big; others were worse off than ever. But there was just no push coming from anywhere. We were all just a bunch of atomized individuals again.

So the closeness I felt driving along with Carrie dozing by my side was a real thing, important to me. I didn't want it ever to end, and yet I knew we had to get to Atlanta soon if we wanted our pay-off. On the road the other sort of companionship I felt all the time was over CB. All those little people scattered across the map looking out for one another were as fast on the burner as a hand on a butter churn.

Carrie's breathing came heavy and hoarse, almost like she had sinus problems, and that was comforting, like having a big soft pussy cat purring next to me.

We by-passed Tuscaloosa and were going to end-run Bessemer and Birmingham, too, by way of Green Pond. Near Siluria I picked up a signal: "This is your Gibbsville React. There's a crash-up on 64. Suggest you consider further alternates."

I quickly got on the mike and told Snowman to come on in as I wondered what to do next.

At last Cletus spoke up, "Just heard the react report. That should give me some time to take another go-go juice break and stick some chowder down my neck."

"We'll be standing by," I hammered back. "Same channel."

I hung up the mike and pulled the Trans-Am to a stop under a clump of oak trees hung with Spanish moss. There was mistletoe growing wild, too, and creeper, and crepe myrtle. Carrie bestirred herself. "Are we in Atlanta already?"

She sat up straight.

"Not so you should worry yourself," I said. "Not quite. Want to stretch those fat little calves of yours?"

Carrie and I got out and went toward the nearby patch of woods. We were no more than four feet apart at any time, and we were walking real slow. Even though I might have liked to hold hands, there seemed to be no real chance that we ever would. Separately, we settled down beneath a large sycamore tree.

We were quiet together, at peace with the slow coming on of the sunlight through the trees and the footfalls of small birds on twigs and dry leaves. A quail was calling to her mate. A squirrel scampered down a bough overhead and leaped across to another. Carrie suddenly became quite animated, as if her whole life history was pouring out of her mouth in one flood.

"I almost married him. Really! Junior! Actually I once married a stockbroker . . . a stockbroker? *Would you be-*

lieve? We were together for two and a half years. It seemed like 20. And now 'almost' with a deputy sheriff. Jesus."

"*You* almost married *that* tub?"

"Naw," she said. "His son Junior. Bet you thought I was still an old maid."

She was smirking. Teasing me, I thought. But I was comfortable with that, too, resting back comfortable against a tree.

"You misjudge me, Carrie. I'm not just some purty face," I explained. "You looked like you been around."

"Coming and going," she said. "But I ain't ever been real bad."

"I never thought you were," I protested. "It was different. You were married."

"And divorced," she added. "Being a single woman after that had its moments. I have this nutty little flat in New York, New York. Pretty. The sun comes in three windows. I'm happy there. Even though it's in a rough neighborhood." She was smiling at me through the mist of her memories.

"Hey," I asked, "know why they call it *New* York?"

"No?"

"Because it's so big," I said.

It wasn't that funny, but she laughed. I watched her, amused, inflamed, but patient all the way.

"What's up now?" I asked her.

She laughed back some more.

"What?" I asked her.

Laughing, she said, "You just give me the giggles."

That was my cue. I moved her way.

"Maybe I can even do better than that."

"Maybe you can't," Carrie said. But, as I withdrew, she added, "On the other hand . . ."

Mouth slightly open, she leaned back on her elbows as I came real close and kissed her. I won't go into any details, on that first contact of our lips, except to say it stiffened my resolve toward her for sure. The moment our lips brushed was a fire all the way down our bodies. If we withdrew, it was for fear of getting scorched.

And there was the road to think of. As we were dallying, Snowman (I later learned) went into this truck stop to call on home to Waynette. He had Fred tied on a long lead around his wrist while he stood in the booth and spoke to the wife and kiddies. When he hung up, this real gruesome-looking biker in leather approached him. "Hey man, this your goddamn mutt?"

Cletus says he owned up, figuring he could handle just about anything.

"Well he just bit me," the biker said.

"*Fred*? Impossible. C'mon man," Cletus told him, "Fred don't bite."

Cletus began walking back toward the counter for his burger and fries, easy on the burnt stinkers.

The biker declared, "I just said to you the mother bit me."

"He's got better taste than that," Cletus said.

People in the diner started laughing, as no doubt they should have, but that biker had a real bad case of low self-esteem, I guess, and didn't like folks laughing at his expense. He shot out his booted foot toward Fred as if to kick him hard between the ribs. The hound leaped back and growled, baring his teeth, as much scared as ferocious.

"Hey, back off," Cletus said. "Man's got no right kicking my dog."

"Whoever said," went the biker. "This animal's got rabies for all I know. It should be put to sleep."

Another biker buddy joined him too. "Let's just put the poor little fella outta his misery."

Now Cletus is well over six-and-a-half foot tall and in most brawls I'm taking short odds on him, but this time the first biker took a pool cue off the wall rack and started toward Fred. He poked the thing hard at the hound as if he would blind him or disembowel him or even worse, so Cletus whirls and slams his fist into the biker's pock-marked face, blowing him against the juke box. The record skipped. It happened to be Merle Haggard's recording of "Okie From Muskogee," Cletus swears, and it came on as loud as the B-52s over Hanoi some years back.

This brought all the other bikers in the diner to their feet and coming at Cletus. He soon saw he was right in the middle of a powder keg—with no way out. He backed up toward the pool table and grabbed his own cue.

"En garde," Cletus said. He swung the pool cue like a musketeer.

So the bikers split and started to move around him. He couldn't keep an eye on all of them at the same time. When they made their final rush—three from the front, two from the side, and one over the top of the pool table—Cletus nailed the biggest of them with a pool cue to the pecan sack. As this big lug doubled over with pain and worry about the family jewels, another leaped over the pool table and crashed into Cletus from behind—knocking his pool cue away. Then another one made his rush and got a steel-toed Frye from Cletus to the vital parts.

But then two others nailed him from each side and it was all over. No use in fighting back anymore when your hands are being held behind your back. Cletus used his feet as catapults and tried to break loose, but Pockmarks picked himself up from the juke box, strolled over, and let him have it twice in the groin, and then as Cletus doubled over and fell onto the ground, he got it another time in the *kishkes*.

Cletus had trouble breathing. The pain was something fierce, too, when he landed with a thud face down and ass up in the gravel. Then they grabbed poor old Fred and threw him out after Cletus.

Hot damn. Old Cletus slowly pulled himself up to his feet again, checked out all his various parts, and began walking with Fred on the limp right alongside him.

The gasoline attendant was waiting for him with a bill for $23.84. Cletus paid and even accepted a bag of vittles from the counterman, who came outside to offer his solicitations.

Cletus had something else on his mind, and he was bound to do it right and white. He settled into the cab of his truck and fired up the big 18-wheeler and put her into gear. He told me he was even smiling, from here to Nashua, New Hampshire. As the big rig leaped forward under Cletus' gloved hands, he had it roar right down on a long line of parked, solid chrome choppers, Harleys, and BMWs close together like white on rice. He rolled right over all of them one by one, like tenpins.

Crunch.

Complete wrecks. Chrome. Mirrors. Fenders. Tires. All crushed and mutilated. A slaughtering of the hogs. Those bikes would never ride again. Just as it should be, too. Even the boy who pumped gas yelled at Cletus, ''Far out! Far freaking out!''

I certainly never would want to argue with that one.

XIX

Hagar's Way

At that same moment, Carrie and I came out of the woods together and by then everything had changed, changed utterly, and yet it hadn't. The terrible beauty that was born between us when our lips touched welded us together in other ways, too. We went into that hazel wood because a fire was in our blood, but now with such ashes hauled and dampened, we wandered out together holding hands.

From ten paces away we heard poor, battered Cletus trying to signal us on his CB: "Bandit I, bring yourself in. Stop playing with yourself, Bandit I and bring yourself in. Do you copy?"

I reached for the press-to-talk mike. "We're listening, Snowman. Back."

Cletus was talking through a mouthful of sloppy Joe. Sounded like mish mash to me, but Carrie deciphered as how my old chum had run into a little fisticuffs at the eatum-up-stop.

"You okay?" I demanded.

"Just fine," he said. "But we blew 20 minutes. Let's move."

We came rolling down the rest of the mountain, and the golden apple of the sun was blazing next to the silver apple of the moon. Over the radio Doug Kershaw played "Alabama Baby."

Carrie began to talk again about her history.

"I've known many men in my time. Some I have truly cared for and others not. The loss was mine, I suppose."

"I suppose."

"Once in Boston," she said, "I saw a man run over by a steam roller."

"Gross," I exclaimed.

"Just wanted to check if you were really listening to me," she grinned impishly. "Actually, my heaviest relationship was with a rock singer named Rambling Bobby Holt. We were together nearly eight weeks," she went on, "four whole fortnights. I thought for sure he was it. Mr. Right."

"And?"

"Plainly he wasn't. One day," she caught her words tightly and spat them out again with a stifled sob, "I came home and found him taking a shower . . . with another girl . . . and her sister."

"Nothing like wiping the slate clean," I told her, because I wanted her to know the past didn't matter. She couldn't upset me with the past. Unless she had worse things than that to tell.

Carrie said, "The man I saw run over by the steam roller—he was real nasty. Shouldn't really speak ill of the dead, it's not right, but that one never did learn how to treat me right."

If we hadn't been on the lam like that, the Lord knows what I might have said. But there was the road to worry about, Atlanta up ahead, and Buford grinding along somewhere behind us. He'd dropped his whole exhaust system somewhere on the way so that, they say, you could hear him in Memphis when you were in Natchez. Still he persisted: mean as a moth. One ornery toad of a sheriff he was.

About 50 miles from the Georgia state line a passing trucker stopped me and handed me a note from Ginger.

Dear Bandit Pandit, not everything always works out like we hope things to, and I am now as free as the driven rain again. Come see me sometimes if you're lonely. I sure am, and I remember the way you pushed me in youı Ozurk swing.

Ginger . . .

Well, I wasn't really interested, and I didn't want to leave inflammables like that lying about anywhere (especially since the lady had threatened to have me pole-axed in her last communication). So, though I wondered what had gone wrong with her and Miner Loomis, I decided not to try to get too nosey. Maybe that carbide lamp just plain lost its wick. I drove on, a wanted man, but not always wanting those who said they were wanting me.

About 25 miles before the Georgia state line, somewhere between Esteboga and Abernathy, I got on the CB and gave out my twenty to one and all, asking for a CB report all down the rest of Route 85. A very hot female voice came back at me, full of the aroma of incense, colored candles with dim lights maybe, patchouli, and stained glass contact paper over the windows.

A voice like sex between consenting adults. "This is Foxy Lady, Bandit. Sweety, what can I do you for?"

That voice gave off the aroma of Old Grandad, platinum hair, and see-through negligees from Frederick's. It had the sound of bedsprings squeaking to stereophonic Allman Brothers blues. "We heard you were coming our way, lover man, and decided to take care of the Bears for you. A little personalized service."

As I whipped down the highway I noticed a pink mobile home set way back from the roadway with a lady in a black lace mumu sitting out in front. There was a very long CB antenna sprouting from the roof and two Alabama State patrolman's sedans parked in front. I just had time to see the lady wave as I went whipping past, and then I heard that sexy whisper back at me again, "Two on one may not seem fair Bandit, but it's all in the line of duty and right now duty calls."

"Be good to yourself, Foxy Lady. Send me the bill."

"Better yet," she said, "why don't you drop by and pay up in person?"

"Maybe," I said, "I'll catch you yet, on the flipside."

Little did I know Buford had caught up to us sufficiently by then that he would be flipping channels, looking for a clue to my twenty.

He musta heard the Foxy Lady tell me, "At the pull-off on Marker 86. You know the place. A pink trailer. Drop on by sometime, Bandit, and stay sweet."

"I'll be there," I said, joking right back at her. And added under my breath: "Someday sweety."

Well Carrie must not have heard the latter, because she was smiling at me shaking her head when I added, only for her benefit naturally, "Believe me, sweet luv. She's got a heart of gold."

"I believe it," she said dryly.

We were now less than 20 miles from Georgia, just two blurs on the highway, Bandit I and II respectively. I thought of Ginger and how she wore underpants monogrammed with the days of the week: Monday, Tuesday, Wednesday. She just didn't have Carrie's class. A bit of a frump too, even though you could heat her up like last night's stew.

Carrie was different. No hype there. A woman of real feelings.

I was getting all dewy-eyed again just thinking about her next to me and asked, "What are you gonna do when you get back home?"

"Go to bed," she said dryly again.

"Real good idea."

". . . *and sleep* . . . for a week," she added hastily. "*Alone* . . . I guess."

"*Alone* . . ." I swallowed hard.

"Stay sweet," she added then and abruptly, impatiently, leaned across the seat and gave me, not a serious kiss, but a sort of sopper on my cheek. She ran her fingers through my topper.

We were somewhere near Pig Creek; you could almost smell its deep funky smell of rotten blossoms and wood shavings. Good old Southland with its smells. No place like it anywhere in the world. Savannah with its stink of brackish waters; and inland Pig Creek with its aromatic spit of land all up and down the border between where we were and Georgia.

An Alabama State trooper was parked by the roadside

swatting flies with his mate when we skedaddled past. Lickety-split he jumped into his car, hit the siren, and took off. Right behind us, and losing ground, but there nevertheless.

A six-truck convoy was moving up ahead of us. The rear truck was hauling pusholine. Several small sedans were between me and the fire water wagon.

I got on the mike with a breaker: "*Breaker Breaker*, this is Bandit I. Coming up on portable gas station. Do you copy? Propane in a Thermos?"

A voice from nearby challenged me: "Bandit, this is Mr. B, and I'm gear-jamming this rolling refinery. You also got another Smokey on the rubber?"

"What else?" I asked. "Can you give me cover Mr. B?"

"Come ahead on, Bandit," he urged, "and we'll slip you into the rocking chair just like you were on the Talaposa swing. Copy?"

"Copy. For sure,' I said.

Blue lights swirling overhead, the tropper was weaving in and out of traffic after me. I floorboarded it, passed three sedans, and slid back into line like a rosary bead on a string.

Just then a string of oncomings whizzed by. I waited, and then hopped back out into the oncoming lane. Passing another four cars, I headed toward that six-truck convoy. Behind me the trooper passed the same first three sedans and darted back into line.

Reppo deppo I started back out again. It was almost bonnyroo, as I roared up to the convoy on my two back wheels, and those six trucks broke rank, leaving a big opening in the middle wide enough for Terry Bradshaw and two running backs running interference to move through. As I passed the first three trucks, I was slipping sideways back into the convoy. Slipping and sliding, as they say, so those trucks could all close ranks around me.

I thought of steel and black leather then and of nights along the damp neon-lit wharfs of Houston or maybe Mobile. The taste of metal in my mouth and rust reminded me of girls I'd known who always dressed in black leather with silver crucifixes hanging down between their breasts, and gangs of tough Mexican kids near Brownsville or New Orleans or

Biloxi. Don't ask me why. It was just an association I had, like the smell of fish or something. A wetness in the air, a smell of fish, police sirens blaring, all reminded me of when I was a young hood just barely making a dollar and on my own for the first time in my life.

I thought of all that now again as I floored it and Carrie screamed with surprise, while those trucks formed a kind of protect-the-livestock circle all around me. Looking through my wide side view, flashback mirror, I could see another trooper come practically up to the back door of the last truck. I wondered if he'd draw on us with something or other, but knew better. We were just breaking speed laws, not causing serious grief to anybody.

The trooper passed truck six and five but just then number four pulled out of the convoy, as if to pass, right in front of that speeding Smokey. His car was forced off the highway onto the shoulder. Then he floored it, passing the convoy and us—unaware that we were hiding next to number four.

So we were in the clear again, or almost. I touched Shanghai with my foot and passed every one of the lead three trucks. The quiet in the Trans-Am once we passed that racket was like white noise. A sudden silence interrupted only by the crackle of my CB static. We had lots of open space before us and behind us.

I quick got on the burner once again: ''Mister B, I don't know how to thank you.''

''Thank me by not getting caught,'' he said. ''Ginger also says to tell you you're a big louse Bandit, but she loves you. Have a good day and a better one tomorrow, good buddy.''

Then I got on the popcorn popper with Cletus to give him advance what for: ''You're about to hit a convoy. Tighten up on your rubber band. The oncoming's clear.''

We were crossing into Georgia as the big 18-wheeler took the oncoming lane. While he let her roll and roared past the pusholine convoy, Cletus gave a long blast on his horn to each of the trucks as he passed, and every truck responded with a big blast back.

Mr. B also told Cletus some minutes later of how he'd

driven past Foxy Lady's place just as poor Buford was leading a naked trooper out of that mobile home at gunpoint. A case of mistaken identity, apparently, as he musta thought he had me. I wonder if he also read the poor man his rights from a Miranda Card and made him "hit it" and spread 'em before he was disabused by somebody or other that he had the wrong fella.

The things some people do out of jumping to conclusions. You just know such people would do the same thing out of stupidity, if given only half a chance. As my old ma used to say, the Lord gives some of us brains and the rest black-eyed peas with ham.

XX

Pushing Through Georgia on the Home Stretch

If you come into Georgia by way of the Opelika-La Grange stretch of Highway 85, you are likely to run into Smokies everywhere you turn. But, as I've already mentioned, just at the last minute some miles back, we'd headed up toward Highway 20, through Heflin as I recall, and into Georgia below Tallaposa and Muscadine, and usually that stretch of the highway is fairly empty. Okey-dokey so far as the Smokies go. Leastways it always was in times past.

This was the final tug on the rubber and as we rounded an overpass with Cletus in the lead, he looked to the right and saw two Georgia State sappers closing in on us.

Carrie was asking me, "What will we do for excitement on our second date?"

"You like the Santa Monica pier?" I asked.

"That's a long ways off," she said.

"So what? We'll go. I'm partial to hot weather."

"I would be kinda partial to something stationary after this," she grinned.

"Sure enough . . ."

Before I could finish, Cletus was on his CB: "Bandit I, let me offer a piece of advice."

"What's that, pardner?"

Cletus said, "Don't take that foot off the hammer, 'cause you got bears about to pour over you like maple syrup . . . or 'make that Karo . . . or Log Cabin,' I'm afraid, if you know what I mean. The real stuff's much too good for them bears."

Before he'd finished, I was glancing through the rear view and there they were, like big fried eggs on the move. Well, as it so happens, I have lots of friends in that part of the state, and one little friend in particular I can always count on. Still, I hesitated making this call on channel 19 for Carrie's sake.

"Do it, Bandit," Cletus called out to me then, "or else you'll surely rue it . . . and explain to your passenger later."

I switched to channel 19: "BREAKER. BREAKER. THIS IS BANDIT TO HOT PANTS. COME BACK."

"WHY SHOULD I?" Her voice was full of sass, just full of vinegar, but familiar. An old friend's voice, I thought.

I said, "I really need your help, sweet thing . . . and," I added, glancing back at the ground-gaining Smokies, "I need it bad."

I'd caught Hot Pants at her hang out, The Thrivin' Drive-in, down off Peachtree, and from all the background noise of country-western, car horns, and general noise and gnattering, I knew the place must be really hopping. I imagined her sitting in her customized Model A with 200 horse under the hood, beaming back at me on the CB, and I really prayed for a little cooperation. Due to friendly memories of former friendly encounters.

Little did I know she was so hard-up she'd turned waitress to make spare change and was working that shift. She said, "I'm on the griddle this afternoon, Bandit, backed up from here to the highway."

"Hot Pants, please," I shot back at her. "In about five minutes I'm going to be flying by with a pack of Smokies on my tail. Can you lock it off behind me?"

No answer.

"What do you want me to do," I pleaded, "*beg*?"

"Yes. Why not?"

"So? I'm begging."

"I want you to know," Hot Pants said, "I'm doing this against my better instincts."

"I owe you a big one, Hot Pants," I said.

"You sure do," she said. Her whisper became husky. "I heard all about that lady you been traveling with. . . ."

I hung up my mike before she could say anything more and hoped for the best.

Carrie was staring at me glassy-eyed. "You actually date a woman who still wears hot pants?"

"That's not why they call her that," I said under my breath.

But I had Smokies to shake off me as best I could. The expressway was fairly empty so I crossed over the center divider before there was any oncoming and proceeded the wrong way down a ramp with both Smokies tagging after me. Then I made the hard right and went back up again, and crossed over the freeway once more, and then hung another hard right onto this grassy slope. One car followed; the other stopped on an overpass to watch the fun.

I started to traverse the hill and the Smokey in pursuit followed and came a cropper against that terrain and flipped sideways, his doors springing open like lawnmower blades as he tumbled out onto the grass unharmed. After that I headed back onto the freeway in the same direction I had started going. But another Smokey, having just arrived from headquarters I suppose, now blocked my glide path.

Again I spun her 180 degrees so I was going the wrong way up the on ramp. The Smokey who'd been waiting for me on the bridge was now coming at me head-on. It was a game of chicken catch-a-Smokey. At the very last split second, that crazy flathead hung a hard left and went sailing right over the railing.

Believe it or not, he came down belly whopping and wheels spinning on the empty bed of this flatbed truck that was heading back to Sheboygan or Detroit for more autos. Nobody hurt: no hits, no runs, no errors on my side either, but as I went down the ramp onto some two-lane blacktop crisscross below, two more Smokey sedans had joined up for the chase, along with a third from the County Mounty's office.

I got busy on the pressure cooker. "Hot Pants . . . this is Bandit. Do you copy?"

"That's a great big ten-four. Come back."

"Coming at you. You ready?"

"Ready, willing, and able. Channel clear."

When I came to the rise of the next hill, I was doing a solid 120. Behind me a dozen more sedans with the Georgia State seal were keeping pace.

Over CB I called out "I'm crossing over right now," and hung a left and slid down the nearest two-lane blacktop. Looking back then I saw it all happen. Beautiful!

As soon as I cleared the intersection, a stream of old junkers and souped-up Camaros and VW bugs with Rolls-Royce grilles just filled the lane behind me, like a big willy roll unwinding. Another long line of similar vehicles was also moving down along the shoulder opposite to us. Those cars filled up all the lanes shoulder to shoulder, and they began to move down the highway, eastbound and westbound, all doing a very conservative law-abiding 55 mph.

Those troopers came roaring down the eastbound lane, only to find the road blocked by teenage traffic forward and back. They were plain stuck, with a little help from my friends. Even the shoulders were stopped up with cars from The Thrivin' Drive-in. All those law-abiding citizens out for a peaceful country ride. Right about then I disappeared around a distant curve.

It was now late afternoon and after a while we'd be having twilight. I grabbed the first opportunity to shoot back onto the highway just ahead of Bandit II. Carrie had been holding her breath all this while, I think, so now she let it out with a sorta pout. "So? Why *do* they call her Hot Pants?"

Cletus came back on the burner again, thank God: "Just four miles to go, good buddy."

So we really were Atlanta-bound and were going to make it just as sure as margarine turns yellow.

I told Carrie then, with love in my voice, "They call her Hot Pants same reason I call you Frog."

"Why is that?" she pouted.

"Because I just said so, Froggy."

So that's the way that happened and we both really

couldn't help smiling over it a little, lewdly and shrewdly, because I think Carrie knew if a man gives a woman a pet name, he ain't that interested in someone else, some old flame, let's say, bygones being bygones. The trouble was we weren't off the nickel quite yet. The State sent out a search and destroy mission of State helicopters and they were hanging like big chandeliers overhead giving fire control signals to all the rest of those State trooper battalions.

We were driving like crazy; I think I darn near pushed Mario Andretti's old mark on the flatout. Behind me was virtually every type of law enforcement in the state: State troopers, local sheriffs, County Mounties, all blowing down the expressway, blue, red, yellow, orange, and chartreuse lights swirling.

Now we could also see the immense structure of the Southern Classic track, our destination, looming in the near-not-far.

The sounds of the sirens and the whooshing of the choppers were deafening.

Carrie said, "Talk about being popular."

I was speechless. Up ahead at the entrance to the Fairgrounds under the huge billboard announcing "The Southern Classic" was an additional greeting party: ten cop cars blocked the entrance gate to the stadium proper. Twenty big-mutha cops formed a line in front of their vehicles. The TV people had moved outside with their cameras, too, for a make on the final arrest.

I was losing my courage. A man can only push himself so far. After a while even nerves of steel begin to rust with nervous perspiration.

Over CB I told Cletus, "Hate to say it, man, but I think it's over. We gave it a hell of a shot, but now it's time to lay down our hand and go off to the promised land behind bars."

"Are you loco, pardner? We've come this far." Fred was also barking like crazy. "Not to worry," Cletus said.

"Yeah, but . . ."

"When we agree to do a job, we do it. Right?"

"But they are waiting for *me*," I pointed out, "Burl Milton Bandit. They don't even know Cletus Snow exists."

"Well they sure are gonna," he said. "Now move aside, good buddy, 'cause I'm a-coming through."

Cletus really put it to the floor. The huge 18-wheeler took the final bullet lane and bit down hard and passed me, almost blowing off my doors. He roared right at the race track gate, hammer down, stacks open, horn blaring, no more nice guy, and with me eating dingleberries off his tail. Behind us maybe two or three hundred yards, 27 bubble gum machines were lighting up the Georgia countryside.

The cops saw 18 wheels of terror roaring downhill full tilt toward them. Some ran off to their cars as fast as they could and skedaddled. Others skittered away on foot. Fast as they could. Period.

Cletus took aim at the gate and cut right through the remaining posse, sending cars reeling like peewees in a marble game: higgledy-piggledy, mumbly-peg. It would be like harpooning the great white whale or a killer shark to catch him now.

"CALL ME SNOWMAN," he cried out over CB as his big rig blasted through the entrance gate, sending out big shards of shrapnel and timber in all directions.

Then I heard him yell, "Let her rip." He pressed a button and a big air bag opened inside the cab of his truck, like an enormous white balloon. Concussion-proof, he headed for the track itself, smokestacks blasting. I came roaring through right after him with my fog lights blazing.

"Son of a bitch! That crazy coot. He made it!" Big Enos Burdette is supposed to have cried out to all his pals when he saw us, through the lenses of his binoculars, coming at him.

He's also supposed to have said, "Done for a dime. Damned for a quarter. I'll fix somebody's ass before I pay off that crazy wild madman."

Be that as it may, all the stock cars with big white numbers on their sides were still whipping around the curves like greyhounds chasing rabbits when Snowman and me plowed a path across the infield and roared onto the track like gangbangers.

"Hot damn," went Enos then, as we pulled up right in front of the whole Burdette family along the infield.

Swerving to avoid our parking spots, stock cars slithered and sailed up in the air, this way and that, avoiding collisions. The flags went down and the race was abruptly called off for that day. The doors of our car and truck flew open and we all raced out and headed for the Burdette family cluster. I was first and I slid to a halt in front of Big and Little Enos Burdette with a can of Coors in either of my hands.

I handed a brew to Big and asked, "What time you got?"

He looked defeated, though all he said was, "One minute after."

"Damn your hide, Enos Burdette," I said, "but we're almost ten minutes early."

I could see Smokies gathering at the upper gate and glanced at my watch again. "I have a big problem up there. It's down to a matter of money and a road out of here."

Quick as a flash, Big Enōs handed me a set of car keys and pointed toward his obnoxious big white Texas Caddy pimpmobile with the granite-colored roof. "There's your back road out, son, and it ain't no dirt track. Now on the money thing," he added, "you feel like going double or nothing?"

"Not necessarily," I said, moving for the Caddy quick.

"All you got to do," Big Enos said, "is run up to Boston and get me a little soft clam chowder. The white . . . with potatoes and leeks. Know what I mean?"

"Deal!" I said, suddenly ravished myself.

"You got 18 hours," Big Enos said. "How's that?"

I felt like saying he could go stick it for all I cared, potatoes and all, but Snowman, seeing my fierce expression, stopped me with a bout of his own enthusiasm. "Bandit and Snowman, Snowman and Bandit. Together again."

"Call you tomorrow," I said.

"Terrific," Carrie put in. "Boston is almost as civilized as New York, New York during certain seasons of the year."

As the first of the police started in to the race track area, we all dove into the Caddy and pulled away again. I could see Big Enos making book with his son when we drove off. Could even read his fat slobbery lips moving: "Twenty to one I break him this time."

So Little Enos said, "Gimme Bandit for $500 . . . at those odds."

In the Caddy we almost seemed invisible. Nobody thought to recognize us. We picked our way through the swarm of police on foot and in cars all headed for the infield. Negotiating the Fairgrounds exit, we saw a smoking hulk with not much left on a chassis except a driveshaft and a steering wheel. Of course, that was Sheriff Justice's car on its very last legs, or should I say wheels. It was blocking the exit, my exit out, so I got out and walked right over to it and went up to the front end of the car and lifted it out of our way. Buford was sort of setting in it all the while, only he really didn't seem to recognize me either. So disconsolate, like he was still in shell shock.

So I said, "Never you mind, sir. I'll fix this," being very gentle and solicitous toward him. There was a piece of fender still hanging on by a thread of metal. With two fingers I snapped it off and threw it on to one side on the dirt.

Then Justice came out of his wreck and actually started talking to me. He looked almost as battered as his car but none the worse for wear in the long run: just dirty and stinky and tattered, as if he'd dressed up for a parade of ragmen. He looked at me and uttered a gasp of breath so piteous and profound. "You may not believe me, stranger," he said, "but I'm a sheriff."

"Absolutely," I said. "I know that. I can tell . . . from your badge . . . and your car . . . and your face."

"Some crazy madman I been chasing from Texarkana," he said, "he musta got away. I followed him all the way here." He squinted at me real shrewdly. "*Don't I know you?*"

"Not so to speak," I said. "Not for my money's worth anyway . . . anyhow." I whistled real loud at him. "*Texarkana all the way to here? That'd be a big long trip.*"

"It was worth it boy," he said. "Worth all of it. I got that CB-jockeying lunatic on a hundred counts of . . . a whole lot of things, including . . ."

"Just no respect for the law nowadays," I interrupted, "some people . . . they . . ."

We were moving through this fresh green breast of the new world, this Eden together in the darkness. And as we traveled north the CB crackled with the news and rumors of all kinds about a fella name of Bandit.

"BREAKER BREAKER THIS IS BANANA PEEL."
"YEAH BANANA PEEL GO HEAD ON."
"DID YOU HEAR THEY NAILED THE BANDIT?"
"YEAH I HEARD BUT THEY WON'T."
"BREAK BREAK THIS IS FAST ED. THEY COULDN'T NAIL HIM. I HEARD THE SUMBITCH WAS IN ALASKA."
"BREAK. THAT'S A NEGATORY. I'M THE BLACK KNIGHT AND I'M HERE TO TELL YOU THAT OLE BOY IS IN EUROPE FRANCE SOMEWHERE. . . ."

Which only goes to prove, I think, that you can fool some of the people all of the time and some of the people none of the time. The rest ain't worth getting dressed for. You copy?

10-Roger.

Bandit

Author's Afterward

Some men take the law into their own hands and are eventually punished.

Others are taken by the law for eventual punishment and manage to escape.

True courage is knowing the right of way at over 55 mph.

Men do what they must do, and very often they will have a light beer when they're finished.

On the move some people run out of gas, and others use credit cards.

Injustice is an exit ramp leading nowhere.

In writing *Smokey and The Bandit* I have been intensely aware of the necessity to encourage the further development and exploitation of domestic crude.

D.H.

El Dorado
Arkansas

A Glossary of CB Slang

aces—superlative
aces over full house—pretty close to the tops
airhead—dummy
back it down—stop transmitting
bear—police of any kind
beaucoup jack—lots of cash
benny chasers—amphetamines
biker—one who drives a hog
bodacious—clear reception of signal; right on target
bonger—gear shift
bootrest—accelerator
bulldog sitting on your bonnet—truck emblem
burner—CB radio
burnt offering—total wreck
carton of eggs—rhyming slang for legs
chigger—a bug of Southern origin that gets under the skin and causes swelling, itch, and much discomfort
cockleburrs—amphetamines
copy—follow, dig
cornshucker—a rube, a rural type, a hayseed
County Mounty—sheriff's dept.
cow pies—dung, manure

Cowton—Ft. Worth, Texas
cracker—refinery
the creeper—lowest gear, or combination of gears to get extra power
deadhead—as verb meaning to return home quickly without stopping
donkey—trail or tail
double nickel—55 mph
ears on—CB turned on
ERA—proposed Constitutional amendment by which women are to be granted equal pay for equal work, among other rights guaranteeing equality of status
eyeball—meet
fixin' to go—preparing to leave
flaky—slightly nuts
foot touching China—hitting the pedals hard
four-ten—10-4, insistently
fubarred—fouled up
fuzzballs—peaches
galore galore—explanation of immensity, superlative
geegaw—ass
giggle juice—gas
give a hissy—throw a fit
go-go juice—gas, fuel
going home hole—high gear
gollee bum—exclamation
grains—amphetamines
green—clear
gross my twiddling antennae—freak me out
handle—moniker, calling name
higgledy-piggledy—in great disarray
hog—motorcycle
hoosgow—jail
I'God—in the name of the Lord
jammers—breaks
Locoweed Valley—a high, grassy area of Texas
machs nix—means nothing (German; Army slang)
Mile High City (or town)—Denver, Colorado
modulating—chatting
nookey—sex

oil burner with a load of hanging beef—a meat truck
on the dodder—limping along
pedal to the metal—foot on accelerator
pincher—a bottom man
propane cooker—a lot of hot air
pusholine—gas
putas—prostitutes
Quake City—San Francisco
queer for the hind—a bottom man
quid—tobacco
RCH—red cootie hair
red eye—country whiskey
red man burleigh—chewing tobacco
rigor mortis—a stiff wheel
scrambled egg—gold braid
semis—18-wheel trucks
shake some trees—front vehicle in convoy playing lookout
Sharktown—Long Island
side view flasher—a truck mirror extending out from the cab of an 18-wheeler
skittering and skedaddling—slipping and sliding
slappers—windshield wipers
slow boatin'—slowing down
Smokey—police of any kind
stacks—exhaust pipes pointing vertically up from the cab of 18-wheel diesel
static sticks—antennae
the strange (chasing strange)—unfamiliar women (going after new women)
streaking—going full speed
sugar britches—sweetie
Swabby Town—San Diego, California
swinging pork—swine carcass, a hanged man
10-4—hello, positive, yes, OK, I understand, Do you follow me?, What?, Definitely
ten pounder—excellent reception
ten roger—message received
Thermos bottle—milk tanker, tank truck
They Lord—meaning "good Lord" approximately
three-car shortie—a little train

throwing a shoe—a flat tire
transmitting—talking a lot
Trash City—San Angelo, Texas
trick babes—prostitutes
White Rock ad—pretty winged naked girl next to a pond

ABOUT THE AUTHOR

DELMAR HANKS is a freelance writer who lives in El Dorado, Arkansas. As a hobby, he raises Malamute puppies, and is a driving safety instructor. He has published many books under a variety of pseudonyms. Under the name of John Howland Spyker, he is the author of *Little Lives* (of the people of Washington County, New York.) He has also written journalism and poetry for numerous magazines as Erik Pearl and Antoinette Messerschmidt. As Richard Elman, he has written ten novels including *The Breadfruit Lotteries*, *Fredi & Shirl & The Kids*, *An Education In Blood*, *Lilo's Diary*, and *The 28th Day of Elul*. A novelization he wrote with Richard Alan Simmons as Michael Lasker for the NBC-TV series "The Gangster Chronicles" won The Longy Zwillman Memorial Award of Elberon, New Jersey. He is also the co-author with Paul Schrader of the novelization of the film "Taxi Driver." Hanks has two beautiful daughters. His wife is a teacher of women's studies and sometimes assists him on novelizing projects. His friends call him "Brugge."